NORTH *to* BENJAMIN

Also by Alan Cumyn

Tilt

The Secret Life of Owen Skye

After Sylvia

Dear Sylvia

Hot Pterodactyl Boyfriend

NORTH TO
Benjamin

WITHDRAWN

ALAN CUMYN

A Caitlyn Dlouhy Book
Atheneum Books for Young Readers
New York   London   Toronto   Sydney   New Delhi

ATHENEUM BOOKS FOR YOUNG READERS

An imprint of Simon & Schuster Children's Publishing Division

1230 Avenue of the Americas, New York, New York 10020

ATHENEUM BOOKS FOR YOUNG READERS is a registered trademark of Simon & Schuster, Inc. Atheneum logo is a trademark of Simon & Schuster, Inc.

For information about special discounts for bulk purchases, please contact Simon & Schuster Special Sales at 1-866-506-1949 or business@simonandschuster.com.

The Simon & Schuster Speakers Bureau can bring authors to your live event. For more information or to book an event, contact the Simon & Schuster Speakers Bureau at 1-866-248-3049 or visit our website at www.simonspeakers.com.

Interior book design by Tom Daly

The text for this book was set in Adobe Caslon Pro.

Manufactured in the United States of America

1018 FFG

First Edition

2 4 6 8 10 9 7 5 3 1

Library of Congress Cataloging-in-Publication Data

Names: Cumyn, Alan, 1960– author.

Title: North to Benjamin / Alan Cumyn.

Description: First edition. | New York : Atheneum Books For Young Readers, [2018] | "A Caitlyn Dlouhy Book." | Summary: Summary: Eleven-year-old Edgar and his mother move to Dawson, a town in Yukon, Canada, for a new start, but when Edgar fears his mother's destructive behavior will force them to leave, he turns to a dog named Benjamin to help him stop the worst from happening.

Identifiers: LCCN 2017039210

ISBN 9781481497527 (hardcover) | ISBN 9781481497541 (eBook)

Subjects: | CYAC: Mothers and sons—Fiction. | Family problems—Fiction. | Alcoholism—Fiction. | Dogs—Fiction. | Moving, Household—Fiction. | Dawson (Yukon)—Fiction. | Canada—Fiction.

Classification: LCC PZ7.C9157 No 2018 | DDC [Fic]—dc23

LC record available at https://lccn.loc.gov/2017039210

For my father,
who urged me to go north,
and for my mother,
who keeps the home fires burning

CONTENTS

FLIGHT

IT WAS A SMALL AIRPLANE, AND EDGAR WAS small inside it. The airplane throbbed; he throbbed. He was in an aisle seat, with little to see. So he was thinking about Benjamin, the dog he was going to be looking after in the new place, and what conversations they might have. Edgar had never had to care for a dog, but Benjamin sounded like he would be a good friend, just from his name—soft fur, big paws, eyes that would love a boy no matter what.

Edgar's mother had mentioned Benjamin at the beginning of telling him that they were leaving, as if this were all going to be a big adventure with a lovely dog at the end of it.

Roger, who could be fierce, had cried when he'd heard Edgar's mother's plans. Roger used to poke Edgar hard in the chest sometimes with two fingers to get his attention. Probably Roger didn't mean to hurt him; probably he didn't know his own strength. And probably he didn't know about Edgar's mother, her history, how she would just leave when something no one else could taste turned sour.

Or—when she just got tired, or scared. When something spooked her.

So now, on the airplane, Roger wasn't there. Yet he had given Edgar a camera. And across from Edgar was a boy who, for a moment early in the flight, had looked as if he too might poke Edgar hard in the chest. So Edgar had pulled his ears back, not wiggled them really, just used his ear muscles to stretch his cheeks flat and make himself still and invisible. He had learned the trick from Roger, from being around him, from not wanting to be noticed.

The tough boy was sleeping now, snuggled up against his mother, who was also sleeping, her long black hair falling against her boy's cheek. The boy's mouth was opened slightly. His hair too was beautifully black against the caramel of his skin. And this was the funny thing: now that Edgar had a camera, so much of what he saw looked like it should be a picture.

Edgar's own mother was staring out the window. Every so often she said, "Edgar!" and he would strain against her and try to see. If he were in his mother's seat, he would probably capture the snowy white peaks of the mountains he knew were out there. But right now he wanted to take a picture of the sleeping boy.

Edgar stretched down, pulled up his knapsack. One of the zippers was broken, so he used the other. The camera was underneath his underwear and an empty bottle that he hadn't bothered to fill with water at the airport in Whitehorse that morning. He wished now that he had some water, because they had missed breakfast. It would be good to sip on something and not feel so hungry.

His camera was heavy, a Nikon. Roger had shocked him with the gift. Sometimes Edgar and his mother left in a hurry in the middle of the night, but this had been a cold sort of leaving, in the day, with everything plain. Roger's cheeks had been wet. He'd been holding himself, but Edgar had known it would not work. When his mother got around to leaving, there was nothing you could do to change her mind.

Edgar knew only what Roger had told him about the camera. In the dim light the flash might go off, and the boy might wake up and come after Edgar. There was a setting you could use if you did not want a flash. But which one was it? Maybe the one just below automatic. The boy snuggled closer into his mother's hair. He was starting to drool.

Edgar zoomed in a little bit, to get the boy's face. He pressed the button halfway to focus. Then click. No flash. He opened up the screen to look: blurry.

In low light you had to hold the camera very still. Roger had told him that, too.

Edgar held the camera steadier, even while the airplane shook. Then the boy yawned and opened his eyes. Edgar could not be invisible. He was sitting right across the aisle, pointing a big camera. "Hey!" the boy said, and his mother woke up too.

Edgar clicked. Then he quickly turned off the camera and stuck it back into his bag. He could feel the boy glaring at him. Edgar pulled his ears back again. He became part of the seat.

"Edgar?" his mother said. The airplane began to bounce. Edgar clutched his bag on his lap and shook in his seat, held in by the belt. The other boy clung to his mother, and the flight attendant gripped her seat tighter but did not look alarmed even when the wings shook so much, they seemed to be flapping.

Then the plane was heading down. A little fast? No one else seemed concerned, but Edgar's mother squeezed his hand so hard, he had to make his own hand soft, soft, almost disappear in her grip, so that it wouldn't hurt too much.

"Almost there, baby," she whispered to him in the voice that he liked the most. There were more bounces, but it was over soon, and they were on the ground.

Suddenly everyone crowded into the squashed aisle, so Edgar stayed seated, clutching his bag. The angry boy stood over him, glaring. Finally the line moved and Edgar rose. Cold air rushed in from the open door at the back of the plane.

There were plenty of other boys on the plane, but Edgar was smaller than everyone else, as usual. At the door Edgar braced himself because the flight attendant looked like she wanted to pat his head. But she didn't. The steps to the ground were metal. Edgar had to fumble in his pockets for his mittens before he held on to the handrail. The cold air felt like a smack in the face. He was careful on the stairs, and did not look around until he was safely on the ground.

Snow-covered hills, bright white. A long empty run-way. The terminal looked like a few wooden boxes you might use for now, while you were building a real airport.

The line of passengers stretched out, and then, like an accordion, it bunched up again at the door of the far-thest of the boxes. Edgar wasn't being careful by then, and he ended up standing right behind the angry boy. Edgar expected him to turn, maybe even to pucker his cheeks and spit. Yet the boy did not move. Still, somehow, Edgar felt his legs were not underneath him anymore. He was free and floating and *bam*! He hit the ground, his hip first, then his elbow.

If this had been the schoolyard—almost any schoolyard—whoever had tripped him would've kicked him maybe too, and Edgar would have tried to roll away. But adults were standing all around them. The boy with the caramel skin was just turning around now.

And Edgar's mother had missed it. "Edgar! Careful. It's slippery!" she said.

"I know." Edgar got up. Who had tripped him?

Then from behind: "I saw what you did, Jason!" It was a skinny girl in a parka, with large brown eyes. Who was Jason? Right next to Edgar a tall, blond, strong-looking boy, with an open jacket and no hat or gloves, smirked at the girl.

"That kid was taking pictures of everybody on the plane!" he said. The other boy, whose picture Edgar *had* taken, didn't seem angry at all now, just amused.

"Last I heard, it's not against the law to take pictures," the girl said.

Then the line moved inside the small, boxy building that was already full of people, families waiting. The girl said directly to Edgar, "Don't worry about Jason Crumley. He's a jerk anyway."

Edgar didn't know what to say. His neck was roasting. Crumley had moved far enough away, across the room, that he couldn't pull another dirty trick.

"Are you new to Dawson?" the girl asked. "Where are you staying? We get a lot of people but usually not till summer. My mom lives in Whitehorse—I was just visiting with her—but I'm based here in Dawson. My dad's coming to pick me up. Do you need a lift? There's no taxi anymore. The Buick broke, and it was going to be too expensive to get the parts sent up. Is somebody picking you up?"

Her eyes were lively, and her nose was curved, how? As if everyone's nose should be as strong. Her skin was caramel too like the one boy's, her hair blond like the other's. And her teeth were brightly white and thoughtful, somehow. (How could teeth be thoughtful?) Edgar didn't know what to say, which question to answer. His mother knew the details of what was supposed to happen next. They were borrowing a house; there was a word for it. Someone was going to meet them when they arrived.

"We are housesitting," Edgar said finally, when he thought of the term. Then he turned away in a broiling state and examined his boots.

They had to wait for their bags. "Why did you take that picture?" the girl asked.

"I was given a new camera," Edgar said quietly. "I was just trying it out."

"Well, my father's girlfriend, Victoria, who is a professional photographer, told me you should never take anyone's picture if you don't know their name."

Edgar nodded. Was he supposed to ask her name now? Probably, he thought, but he felt unsure, so he pressed his lips together and hummed. Jason Crumley was surrounded by family, but he was staring at the girl as if he wanted to get back at her for speaking up. And *she* looked like she couldn't wait for him to try.

Edgar moved close to his mother, then watched as the little baggage car came up from the runway, the trailer loaded with everyone's things. A man in a parka hoisted the bags off the trailer and shoved them through a small swinging door, and the people crowded closer and pulled aside the luggage that belonged to them.

"Could you get our stuff?" Edgar's mother said. She was paying attention to the parking lot out the window, filled mostly with pickup trucks.

The girl now had drifted away. Edgar wanted to say something more to her, but what? All his thoughts felt gummy. Then Jason Crumley moved toward the bags too. Edgar didn't want to chance another dirty blow, but there seemed little choice. It was such a small room, there was nowhere to hide.

But Crumley didn't bother with him now. He lifted a big red hockey bag onto his shoulders and staggered back through the crowd toward his mom. The other boy, with the caramel skin, also pulled a hockey bag onto his shoulder. *Maybe they're on the same team*, Edgar thought. Edgar's mother's black suitcase arrived then too, and Edgar used all his weight to jerk it away from the growing pile. It had wheels. He rolled it to his mother, who was still eyeing the parking lot.

There wasn't even anywhere to buy coffee, and she had gone the whole morning so far without it.

Not to mention breakfast.

Edgar returned to the baggage pile and pulled out his own knapsack, the purple, perfectly good one that someone had thrown out just two weeks ago in Toronto. Edgar had found it on the street in the garbage and had brought it home, although he'd had no idea he would be using it this soon. Well, maybe he had had some idea. When his mother had gotten that look, when winter had taken over her face, especially when she had eyed Roger that way. Then Edgar had known.

The really long flight, eight and a half hours, had been most of yesterday, starting from Toronto on a much bigger plane. Now they had moved so far north, back into real winter, it was hard to believe it was actually April.

They had just two bags each, a big one and a carry-on

from the plane. Everything else had been left behind: his bed, his drum set, his microscope, his bottle collection, everything. So while other people were still pulling their bags from the pile, Edgar and his mother stood aside and watched. Hockey players struggled with bags and sticks, leaving in large groups. Jason Crumley and his family left too. Gradually the parking lot emptied. Edgar and his mother remained inside but were the last people standing by their bags. Even the airline workers had disappeared.

Edgar had assumed that the lively girl's father had picked her up, maybe when Edgar had been wrestling with the bags. But then she surprised him—she walked out of the women's washroom carrying her own small backpack. "I'm Caroline," she said.

Edgar's mother said, "I noticed you from before. You were awfully nice to stick up for my Edgar." She lowered her voice, although Edgar could still hear her perfectly well. "He doesn't stick up for *himself*," she said.

"Jason's been picking on new kids since, like, forever," Caroline said. And then, sounding very grown-up, she said, "I'm not sure if you've arranged for a ride, but my father is coming to get me and we could give you a lift."

"Someone was supposed to be here to pick us up," Edgar's mother replied. When she unzipped her big bag, looking for something, it exploded with her clothes and bathroom things, which had all been squished in tight, tight. Caroline knelt to help her, so Edgar sat a distance away and took out his camera.

"Don't you bloody well take my picture like this!" his mother said. And then to Caroline she said, "Sorry! I don't usually swear," which wasn't true, entirely. And then to Edgar again: "You promised me."

He *had* promised her: to be normal, whatever that was. To fit in. To be just like every other boy and not make trouble even by being too quiet. To not make a commotion—"commotion" being a word he had learned when he was really small. Also, "commotion" being the property of his mother, hers to make. There was not enough commotion to go around so that he, too, could make some.

Edgar blinked back at her so that she understood—of course he would keep his promise. He just wanted to see what that last photo, of the boy on the plane, looked like. Had Edgar kept his hands still enough?

The boy's mouth was open. One fist was clenched, and the other was holding tight to his mother. His eyes looked like what? Like he had wanted to bash whoever was holding the camera.

In the airport bathroom everything was brown and smelled old. Edgar studied his own face in the mirror. He could not see the camera hanging from his neck, just the strap with the yellow lettering. He pulled his ears back again, tried to disappear in front of himself to see if he could.

In a room like this he would have to turn brown too. His hair was brown already. If he stayed out in the sun, his skin could brown quite a bit.

Like Caroline's and the boy's in the picture.

When he returned to the main room, he saw their bags piled and no one else there. His mother and Caroline were outside by the window. His mother puffed on a cigarette, then clapped her hands together in the cold, looking in the distance. Caroline was talking, talking. Edgar took a picture of the bags—his mother's was not quite closed but had the nose of the hairdryer sticking out where the zipper would not shut.

A sign above the public telephone near the door said DAWSON TAXI and gave a number, even though Caroline had said the taxi was not running. So Edgar went outside and told them.

"It's an old sign," Caroline said. "Believe me, that Buick doesn't go anymore. But my dad should be here soon."

"A guy was supposed to pick us up," Edgar's mother muttered. She blew smoke into the cold air. "It was all arranged."

Edgar looked down the road to where his mother was staring. "Do you remember his name?" he asked.

"Well, that would be something, wouldn't it?" his mother said. "I thought I had it in my book." The book was sticking slightly out of her pocket now.

"Regina's friend?" Edgar said.

"The people who own the house we are borrowing are friends of Regina's sister's boyfriend's parents," his mother said. "Don't say anything. It's all arranged."

She said this last bit in a weary voice. She wasn't only worried about the guy, Edgar recognized. She was also worried about money. They were poor. They didn't have money, or much money, for anything, really. It was a miracle that Edgar had been allowed to keep the camera. But they had moved quickly; maybe there hadn't been time to sell it. His mother had wanted to put a lot of distance between them and Roger. The hotel last night, in Whitehorse, *that* had been a miracle too—after all the long hours of flying from Toronto. Normally, in a new place, they stayed with others. They slept on couches, not on queen-size beds big enough to bounce on all you wanted.

But there was no other place in Whitehorse, and they didn't know anyone.

"Maybe we could walk," Edgar said.

"Oh, brilliant!" his mother blurted. "So much for being a little genius. Anybody could think of that!"

Edgar felt his face burn. He knew he should not look her in the eye.

Caroline waited, then said cautiously, "We *could* hitch." She seemed to like thinking about problems and what to do about them. "Whoever comes by will pick us up for sure. But my dad thinks I'm waiting here for him." She looked down the road as if she really wanted to try walking.

"How far is it?" Edgar's mother asked, as if, actually, they might try after all.

"Only ten miles or so," Caroline said. "We could do it in a couple of hours if we walked fast. But somebody would pick us up long before then."

Edgar's mother threw away her cigarette and went back inside.

"Maybe it's too far," Edgar said softly. He followed his mother. Inside was warm, at least. It was hard not to look at the sign for the taxi and think that maybe it *was* working after all. There were other signs too: posters for something called Diamond Tooth Gertie's, which featured ladies in old-fashioned dresses kicking their legs high all together; and for the Downtown Hotel, "Home of the Sour Toe Cocktail"; and excursions to Bonanza

Creek. Gold panning tours would begin in June. He also saw a poster with a strange picture of a large building that looked like a ship, only it was on land. SEASONAL TOURS OF THE NUMBER FOUR DREDGE, it said.

Caroline joined them inside again. "So, whose house are you sitting for, anyway?" she asked.

Edgar's mother looked away in annoyance, probably because she couldn't remember the name of the family, or possibly had not written it down. So Edgar said, "There's a dog I will be looking after, Benjamin."

Caroline's eyes widened. "You're staying in the Summerhills' place? That's just down the street from us! Benjamin is the Summerhills' dog! I've been looking after him, since they couldn't find a sitter. They're down in Arizona."

"But—" Edgar said.

Edgar's mother interrupted him. "Yes, that's it, the Summerhills. I don't know them directly; it's all through my friend, Regina. But somebody, this fellow who was supposed to pick us up, has the key. He has a funny name, if I remember. I can't quite—"

"Ceese?" Caroline said, shaking her head, as if she knew what Edgar's mother was going to say and yet still could not believe it.

"Yes, that's it, Ceese!"

"He's my father!"

"Well, where *is* he?" Edgar's mother said. "Did he not tell you he was picking us up?"

"I tried calling him," Caroline said. "He's out of range, but that's pretty usual around here. He'll probably show up any minute now."

Finally Edgar got a word in. He said, "*I'm* supposed to look after Benjamin. We're going to be friends!"

Caroline looked at him. "We can all be friends," she said, as simple as that.

TREK

THE MINUTES LEAKED BY, AND NO ONE showed up. Caroline talked to Edgar's mother about her own mother in Whitehorse, who was a lawyer for the territorial government, and how together they had walked the Chilkoot Pass last year, which was not as difficult as everyone said. "You don't have to carry a ton of equipment or anything like that," Caroline explained. Edgar didn't know what the Chilkoot Pass was, but a ton sounded like a lot for a girl and her mother, or for anybody, really.

She talked and talked, this Caroline, about her father's girlfriend, Victoria, who lived across the river in West Dawson, which didn't have electricity, but it had a lot of dogs, and about how Caroline couldn't call Victoria because her truck had troubles, but not to worry, her father would be here, he always was.

But he wasn't, so they started to walk.

Edgar swung his big knapsack onto his back, and his mother put his little knapsack on his front, making him feel like a turtle. It wasn't too cold, and the road was deserted. It was bright, though; he had to squint.

Caroline asked where they had come from, and when Edgar told her, she said, "You came all the way here from Toronto just to housesit for a couple of months? Or are the Summerhills not coming back in June like they always do?"

Edgar's mother was thinking, so Edgar had to answer. "I think if we like it here, then maybe we will look for an apartment of our own."

"Good luck with that!" Caroline said almost gleefully. "Everybody likes it here by June, so it's really hard to find a place to stay. Unless you like camping."

There were no signs. The sides of the road were humpy, covered in snow. Edgar was hoping that when they rounded the curve—it took a long time—then the town would appear, but it didn't.

Ten miles really was going to be a long, long way. If only they'd had breakfast!

Suddenly a truck came up from behind them— *whoosh*! They hardly had time to step out of the way. Edgar's mother turned and raised her hand. "Hey!" Then the truck was by. But it stopped down the road and all

three ran to where a man with a hard face was leaning out
the window. He had very few teeth, and Edgar felt his
mother's hand stiffen around his.

"Going to Dawson?" the man asked.

Caroline said, "Absolutely!"

But Edgar's mother said, *"No,"* almost at the same
time. "We don't need a ride."

"What?" The guy couldn't seem to believe what he was
hearing.

"It's okay," Caroline said. "He's got room in the—"

"We're fine. We're just out for a walk," Edgar's
mother said. "Sorry for the trouble!" She pulled Edgar
and Caroline across the road so that the man would
understand.

"But he's going into town!" Caroline looked stunned.

Edgar's mother stayed quiet and maintained her grip.
Edgar knew—she didn't feel right, and that was that.

The man seemed struck dumb. Then in a minute the
truck was on its way and had soon disappeared.

"We'll get the next one." Edgar's mother wasn't wearing a hat, and her ears were turning bright red, but her
cheeks were white. Edgar remembered a story he had read
about a man and his dog here in the Yukon. It was so
cold, the man's spit froze in midair. Edgar knew it was
not that cold now, but he spat anyway. Both his mother

and Caroline looked at him. Maybe they were thinking he was upset about the truck.

He was more upset about possibly not taking care of Benjamin after all. But Caroline had stood up for him against the bully, and maybe she would be nice about this, too. She wasn't bothered now at all. She had her parka, she had boots with fur trim, she looked like she wanted to walk all day.

Edgar was beginning to feel cold in his toes. That's how it had started for the man in the story too, after falling through the ice and getting wet. His toes lost feeling, then his hands. Edgar opened and closed his fists. It helped a bit when he thought again of Benjamin. Now that he could see what the north looked like, how frozen and wintry it was, he knew that Benjamin had to be a husky dog with a thick fur coat and gleaming eyes. Like the dog in the story, actually. But friendlier.

"This is all going to work out," his mother said then.

"That guy did look freaky," Caroline said, "but I've seen him around. He would've been all right. Anyway. There'll be another truck along soon, I'm sure."

Two ravens perched together at the top of a tall fir tree had a strange barking chat. For a moment Edgar imagined himself up there with the ravens looking down. He would be able to see Dawson, how far away it was.

Caroline was right. Soon enough they heard another vehicle approaching, and this time Edgar's mother started waving and calling out even before they could see who was coming. It was a pickup truck, silvery, and it started to slow as soon as it came into view.

"That's my dad!" Caroline broke into a run.

The truck lurched to a stop, and a big man jumped out. He was wearing a thin jean jacket that was open, his boots weren't even laced up, and he didn't have on a hat or mitts. He swung Caroline around until she was laughing. Then he kissed her and put her down, and walked toward Edgar's mother.

"Are you Stephanie?" His skin was darker than Caroline's and he had a brilliant smile, and gray hair, and brown eyes full of light.

"Yes!" She was sparking on him, just in her brief look. She couldn't help it; it was as if she had a switch she could not keep from turning on.

Caroline's father hesitated—of course he did. Then he seemed to recover. He took Edgar's mother's bags and placed them carefully in the truck, where there was a backseat.

"I'm so sorry to be late. There was some weather coming down the Dempster, really slowed me up. My name is Ceese." He held out a large hand to her in a friendly but formal way. Edgar remembered Roger shaking hands like that too, but not with his mother, with Edgar himself. This man, Ceese, did not seem to even notice that Edgar was there.

"We are freezing," Edgar's mother said in what sounded like a brave voice, as if it were no big deal.

"You didn't tell me you were picking anybody else up!" Caroline said.

"Sorry. Sorry!" Ceese opened the door of the truck and guided Edgar's mother in. Edgar stood and watched while he helped her with the seat belt and shut the door against the cold. Finally Ceese turned to him. He squatted down so that they were eye to eye. "I'm afraid I didn't get your name, sir." Ceese's mouth was serious, but his dark eyes were not.

"Edgar."

He put big hands on both of the boy's shoulders. "I imagine you're having a day you're going to remember the rest of your life."

Edgar nodded at him carefully.

"We'll both make sure your mother's all right," he said.

DAWSON

WHILE THEY WERE DRIVING, CEESE, WHO liked to talk, told them all about the history of this place called the Klondike, where gold was discovered a long time ago and thousands of men scrambled north to try to become suddenly rich. Those large humpy mounds, like enormous white worms lining the side of the road, were piles of river stones left by the dredges, now covered by snow. Those dredges were huge, rock-eating ships that chewed up all the streams and spat out everything that wasn't gold dust. Edgar was tired and hungry, and it was difficult to follow such fantastical stories, until Ceese finally said, "Say, does anyone need some breakfast?"

Edgar's mother, who had stopped even pretending to listen, glanced away from the window, and for a moment

Edgar was hopeful. "We had some earlier," she said finally, which was not true at all.

"The Eldorado has a great breakfast!" Caroline said.

Ceese turned to Edgar's mother. "My treat! I was late coming to get you. Sure glad you didn't have to walk all the way into town. Must've been Caroline's idea."

"I knew you'd probably get us on the way!" Caroline protested.

"We didn't have breakfast," Edgar said then. He tried to find a large voice, but it came out, as usual, pretty soft.

"We didn't have *a lot* of breakfast." His mother flashed him a look, and he pretended not to see it.

"All right, then. You'll be riding into Dawson on an empty stomach, but we'll top you up soon enough!"

The town was not big. For a while they were driving along the highway with steep hills to one side and those mounds and a frozen river to the other. Then they took a bend and saw wooden buildings, none of them very high, and most of them, at least on the main street, were closed. One very old building faced many of the others and seemed to be falling apart, and there weren't many cars, or even a traffic light.

"Plenty to do in Dawson," Ceese said, "but not so much now. Everybody who stayed the winter is just kind of waiting and watching as the days get longer and the snow shrinks. When the ice goes out, though, then you'll see a whole flood of people coming for the better weather." He turned to Edgar again. "Do you like contests? Ever since the gold rush there's been one to guess the exact date and time when the ice breaks up on the Yukon River. If you aren't actively panning for gold, that's another way to make a whole bunch of money real quick!"

As they drove along, Caroline pointed out a large orange marker in the middle of the frozen river, with a wire leading back to one of the buildings onshore. "As soon as that pylon begins to move with the ice, it trips the clock," she said. "May the second. That's my ticket. Two seventeen p.m."

"Climate change has screwed everything up," Ceese added. "Breakup could be a lot earlier than that. It's hitting us here in the north much harder than other places. Everything's turning unpredictable."

He steered them away from the river and parked in front of one of the larger buildings. They walked on a wooden sidewalk and up the stairs into the Eldorado Hotel. It looked old and dirty, but Edgar could smell bacon and eggs even before they got to the dining room.

"This is very nice of you," Edgar's mother said to Ceese when they sat down. She took off her winter coat and shook out her hair. Ceese watched her with a big grin on his face. Edgar knew it was hard for men not to watch his mother. Her black hair, her unexpected eyes—so darkly blue.

An older woman with almost orange curly hair brought four menus. "I'd like the pancakes," Edgar blurted. Then he looked up and realized he had interrupted—Ceese had been saying something to his mother, who was smiling.

"Specialty of the house," Ceese said, switching gears. "Syrup, everything, the works?"

Pancakes were more expensive than just the toast and cereal. Edgar hoped his mother wouldn't stop him. "The works," he said in a soft voice.

It all costs money, his mother said, just in the way she blinked her eyes.

But he's paying, Edgar blinked back.

And Caroline was watching everything. She could talk every bit as much as her father, but she had those big eyes too. She asked for a soft-boiled egg and toast for dipping.

Edgar's mother ordered fruit in a bowl of yogurt, and not even any coffee, which could only have been to impress Ceese somehow. But why did she need to impress him? He was the one who had been late to pick them up.

And there *was* a girlfriend, Victoria. Edgar's mother had clearly heard Caroline explain the situation.

Ceese ordered steak and eggs for himself, and two

side orders of toast, in case anyone was still hungry.

"Are you sure you don't want any coffee?" Ceese pressed Edgar's mother.

"Some orange juice would be nice," she allowed. She looked around, yawned, then covered her mouth.

"So I guess you guys have had a long couple of days of travel," Ceese said. "All the way from Toronto? I heard you had to clear out pretty quick?"

The orange juice came, and Edgar's mother sipped it slowly with her eyes closed. "I was really looking for a change of scene."

"Plenty of scenery here, all right," Ceese agreed.

Edgar's mother sipped a bit more of her juice, and then it was as if she couldn't help herself, she drank it all down. "You know, maybe I will have that cup of coffee after all," she said.

"That's the spirit!" Ceese motioned to the orange-haired waitress, and she brought over the coffeepot. They were not the only customers: a pair of large unshaven men in muddy workboots and dusty overalls were sitting back, legs open, staring at Edgar's mother.

"So I heard you were leaving a tough situation," Ceese pressed, swinging the conversation back.

"You could say that." Edgar's mother's tone meant she didn't really want to say.

"Lots of folks come up here to start fresh," Ceese said. "It's amazing how many people came for a summer twenty years ago, and they're still here!"

"Like my mom," Caroline said in a voice, low like her father's, just to Edgar. "But she's in Whitehorse now!"

Edgar's mother sipped her coffee slowly. "Just a good, peaceful couple of months would be fine."

Finally the food came, and Ceese talked on, a torrent of friendly, soothing words, like water in a stream in the background. He had a story about the dredge, and another about a grizzly bear, and one about a miner who lost his gold, and he talked about the old paddlewheel steamers that used to be the only way to make it up and down the river to Dawson. Edgar listened to it all. The more he chewed his pancakes, the sweeter the syrup tasted mixing in with the bacon. And the more he gobbled the side orders of toast all by himself, going through four little packets of jam and one of marmalade, the less he could hold on to all those stories.

Caroline dipped toast soldiers into her eggs, how exactly? Like she was the queen of breakfast.

Afterward Ceese drove them up the hill past wooden buildings, some of them leaning this way and that, as if tiring over the years. Then they took a right on the last street. "That's our house!" Caroline said, but she was blocking Edgar's view. Then they stopped before a house that seemed to have been built largely below the level of the street. It had a wooden bridge to the front door, almost like a drawbridge from an old castle heading over a moat.

Edgar carried his bags across the planks. There was no moat down below, just snow, but there was a lot of space between the railings, and it would be a long drop. Then he was inside, looking, but the place was cold, empty, and terribly silent. "Where is he?" Edgar asked Caroline.

"Who?"

"Benjamin!"

"At my house still," Caroline said. "It's okay, you don't have to look after him right away. Just get settled."

But soon, yes? Edgar said to her with his eyes.

She nodded a little bit, as if in understanding.

"We'll have to warm the place up," Ceese said. "I imagine they've kept the bathroom heat on." He kicked off his boots, and Edgar did the same. His mother seemed eager for Ceese and Caroline to leave, so she and Edgar could have the place to themselves.

This was what the whole journey had been about, Edgar thought. This was why Roger had been in tears. Edgar almost felt sorry for him for a moment. How could

Roger compete with an empty house like this, so quiet, full of other people's furniture?

"I would love to live here!" Caroline was saying. "The Summerhills really fixed the place up in the last few years. *Retired financial advisers*," she said, under her breath.

It was dark until they opened the blinds, cold even after Ceese turned up the thermostat. There were no hot-air registers, but some sort of hot-water-radiator system that would be slow, Ceese said. Now Ceese and Caroline stood together in the doorway, telling Edgar and his mother where the grocery store was, the post office, which bars would be open, what day the garbage was picked up. Edgar tried to keep it all in his head. The grocery store was down the hill almost all the way to the river. The post office was before that, on Third Avenue. He did not remember the bars because he knew his mother would. Garbage was Wednesday morning.

"Anything else I can get for you? Are you all right for money?" Ceese said.

This last question was something not many people asked, but clearly they were all thinking about it. Ceese looked like he had money somehow. Edgar knew that many of his mother's friends had very little, but every so often someone like Roger came along, who had money sometimes at least.

"Thank you, we're fine," his mother said. She smiled. It looked like a last, hard effort. She really wanted him gone! But he was lingering.

"Because I can help out," he said. "This is the north. We're different here."

Different how? He didn't say.

"Thank you," she said again. "If you hear of any positions opening, please let me know. But we're fine for now."

By "positions" she meant jobs, and by "jobs" she meant waitressing or bartending, Edgar knew, even though she had said she would never do either job again. But things had changed.

"I'll ask around," Ceese said, and his eyes stayed on hers, as if he wanted her to believe that he would.

ALONE

AT LAST THEY WERE ALONE IN THE strangers' house. Edgar went to what would be his bedroom, which was small, in the back, but which, when he stood on the bed, had a fine view of the rest of the town out the rear window. Through his camera lens he saw clusters of low wooden buildings, many of them with snow-covered roofs, and a grid of streets, and in the distance black-and-white hills, where the black was fir trees and the white was snow. The sunlight was different here. He couldn't think of how exactly, except that everything seemed clearer than in Toronto. Certainly you could see more than on a big city street, with all those tall buildings and the cars rushing past. And the snow was so white here, not gray and black slush. Slowly, slowly a pickup truck made its way along one of the main roads, and

Edgar realized it was Ceese's, the only moving vehicle in the whole town.

Was Caroline with him? Where were they going? Maybe to see Victoria in West Dawson, wherever that was. Somewhere without electricity.

Ceese's vehicle moved almost out of his frame. Edgar clicked, then kept looking through his lens. In front of the black-and-white hills in the distance, he realized, that wide white stretch was frozen river. Then . . . the truck itself was on the river ice, winding across. Could people just drive anywhere here? Why didn't the truck fall through? As he zoomed closer, he realized it was a road of sorts, a road on the ice. Edgar watched until Ceese's truck reached the other side and climbed a hill, out of view.

The rest of the house was on two levels. The kitchen and the dining room were together, also at the back of the building, with a picture window that let in a lot of light, and down below, on the second level (down the hill, Edgar realized—the house had been built on a slope) was the biggest room, the master bedroom, where his mother had dumped her bags. It was the newest room too, done over recently. The bed made the ones in the hotel in Whitehorse seem small. "Would you look at this?" his mother kept saying, wearing her little-girl face, like a princess just woken up.

As beautiful as the house was, it was sure slow heating up. Edgar kept his jacket on as he went from room to room. The television in his mother's bedroom covered almost an entire wall. There were photographs too, of mountains and bighorn sheep and sunsets and someone in a kayak beside a killer whale half out of the water looking like your best friend, and shelves and shelves of books everywhere, and sofas to sit on. Even though the place had been empty for a month or so, everything seemed clean.

Was it really theirs?

It felt too quiet; it looked way too neat for any place of theirs. And when, when could he have Benjamin? Was Caroline just trying to keep the dog all for herself until the two months were over?

"We're going to have to keep this place in perfect condition," his mother said in her exhausted voice she had been hiding from Ceese and Caroline.

"Benjamin should stay in my room," Edgar said. He knew enough not to press, not to ask his mother for any more information that she did not have. Instead he mentioned that they should go to the grocery store, and she replied that they would, a little later. She just needed to lie down for a bit. Before she closed the door to her miraculous new bedroom, she hugged him in her strong arms for too long, until he had to let out a breath and she released him.

"Someday you'll just hug me back," she said.

Edgar looked at his toes. Two of them, on his right foot, were peeking through holes in his sock.

"It might be when I'm eighty, but I'm willing to wait!" She smiled again, and Edgar wondered if she would be able to sleep here. She had stopped sleeping in Toronto; that was part of why they had needed to come so far.

He wandered back up to the kitchen, found a pen and a small pad of paper by the telephone, and then started a list of what groceries they might need. Maybe for dinner tonight they would have macaroni and cheese, and make a large batch that would do for the next night too. They could buy sausage to put in it, and if his mother insisted on broccoli, then that, too. But he wouldn't mention it. He wrote down oatmeal and fruit and eggs and butter and bread and milk, all nutritious but not expensive. Without Roger—and without Ceese—they did not have a vehicle, so they would be carrying whatever groceries they bought back up the hill. It wasn't a big hill if you were riding in a car, but Edgar knew it would be harder on foot.

The house was as quiet as a tomb, as quiet as what he imagined a tomb might be: dead, gray air; not even a clock ticking. He pulled out a glossy book of photographs from one of the shelves, being careful to mark its spot so that he could replace it perfectly when he was finished.

The photographs were in black and white, and they were all about the Klondike, which meant the river that met another, bigger river, the Yukon. The Klondike was also what Ceese and Caroline had been talking about in the truck and over breakfast, what all those prospectors had come for: gold by the sackful. But these pictures showed no gold at all, just desperate-looking men in ragged clothes—most with shaggy beards—climbing slopes, posing in front of wooden shacks, crowding the very streets that now were so empty. There was a picture of a dredge, as big as an office building, looking stuck in a creek. And here were men with husky dogs, and here was a woman wrapped in fur, looking hard into the camera, and here was an impossibly long line of men stretching all the way up a mountainside and disappearing beyond the top of the picture.

The Chilkoot Pass, according to the caption. Where Caroline and her mother had walked.

Edgar saw only a few children in the book—a curly haired girl with a doll in a fancy dress; a boy with a tiny rifle, looking at his muddy shoes.

He was feeling sleepy himself. He lay on his new bed with his eyes open. If he dozed now, he knew, his mother might go out and buy groceries without him, and he would be left here alone in the tomb.

She might head for the grocery store but end up in one

of the bars, and who knew when she might come home? She might get work and have to serve drinks right away, and he wouldn't know until the next morning, or if she came home and fell asleep before the sun rose, she might not tell him about the job until she woke up in the afternoon.

He went downstairs again and stood in front of her closed door, listening to the soft fall of her breathing.

Maybe she would sleep just fine here.

He sat against the wall near the door and felt his head nodding, so he allowed himself a short nap, knowing that she could not leave without waking him up.

It was starting to get dark when he awoke, and he felt cold and sore slumped against the wall. His mother's door was still closed. In the small bathroom beside the kitchen he splashed some water onto his face and hair, and used the towel that was hanging there, and shut the tap, which had been dripping, probably a long time.

He walked back to the fridge. A map that was taped there looked old and green, with a lot of wavy brown lines, and some white spaces and blue lines where the rivers were. There was the Klondike winding down from the right, and meeting the bigger Yukon, where Dawson was. West Dawson, across the Yukon, was "abandoned," according to the map, and so were other places: Fort Reliance, Forty

Mile, Boundary, Moosehide. How could Victoria live in an abandoned place? Some of the creeks had interesting names: Bonanza, Bear, Deadwood, Shovel. Some of the white spaces were labeled *tailings*, and Edgar thought of the humpy mounds along the highway.

What the dredge had left behind.

Was this an old, old map? Edgar suddenly wondered. Could some places that had been abandoned before now have people in them again?

(*Any place we have lived*, he thought, *we never go back to again*. That was starting to mean a lot of abandoned places by now.)

Suddenly his mother was standing in the kitchen, her hair long and everywhere, her face tired.

"It's cold in here!" she said. "Is the heat even on?"

Edgar went to feel the radiators—which were warm—and his mother opened the fridge door and swore. "We forgot to do the shopping!" she said. "Why didn't you wake me up?"

Edgar said, "The radiator is on."

"Then why is it still so freaking cold?" She slammed the door, but the fridge did not move even one bit.

"Maybe we could go to a restaurant," he said in a little voice, his disappearing voice.

But she did hear him. "Do you think we can constantly

afford restaurants?" Her hands went to her hair. Then she stubbed her toe accidentally on one of the kitchen stools.

"It's okay, I'm not that hungry," he said.

"No, it's not okay. We have no freaking food!"

She was saying "freaking" instead of something else, and so he knew she was not completely angry. She was trying to be fair.

A little bit fair.

"It's good that you slept, anyway," he said.

He went to one of the lower cupboards and filled a glass with water for her. A few years ago, when he was little, and was quite hungry, she showed him how drinking water—which was free, usually—filled you up and made you forget.

He wasn't sure she would take the glass, but she did; she drank the water eagerly. Then she put the glass down and squeezed her temples with her fingers.

"We can try to find something open. I don't know what, in this tin-pot town. But here we are." She said it as if she hadn't dragged them all the way up here, north of North, saying all along how much better it was going to be.

Edgar poured his own glass of water and drank it down. What was a tin-pot town?

This kitchen had pots hanging from the ceiling, but they were made of copper, and they gleamed like new.

CASSEROLE

EDGAR STOOD BY THE DOOR IN HIS JACKET with his boots on and his hat and mitts, in the low light, waiting. His mother was in the bathroom getting ready, probably fighting with her hair or something. If he leaned forward on his toes, then rocked backward, he wasn't so hungry and he warmed up a bit.

They were going to buy groceries, if they could find some, if any stores were open. But then the doorbell rang, a large, jarring sound that startled him. He opened the door and saw Ceese again, standing with his jean jacket still open and no mitts on, just like when they had met him. Only this time he was carrying something, a casserole dish.

Edgar's mother arrived then, still fussing with her hair. Possibly she had lost her comb in it. "What have you done?" she said to Ceese, her eyes wide. "You shouldn't have!" But she took the casserole anyway. She lifted the lid, sniffed, and made warm noises.

"Victoria had it on hand. She wondered if you might like it. It's moose chili, from the fall hunt. You can eat it now or stick it in the fridge. And I forgot to tell you something about the bathrooms." Ceese then explained that it was important to keep a trickle of water running in the sink and bathtub on the main floor, and they shouldn't be using the downstairs bathroom, since those pipes had been drained for the season.

"Edgar, could you go check the bathroom?" his mother said then. "I think I turned everything off." Edgar didn't say that he, too, had turned off the faucet. But it was easy enough to get things dripping again.

When he returned, Ceese and his mother were still talking in front of the open door. Edgar could feel the house getting even colder, but the two kept talking, his mother now especially, she was so thankful about dinner. She went on about Toronto, how frenetic life had been there. She used the word three times, "frenetic," and Edgar thought it sounded like "frantic," so maybe that was what his mother meant. She had been frantic sometimes, her face red and fearful, her eyes especially lost. Maybe that was what "frenetic" meant: the way she became just before running away.

Finally his mother asked Ceese if he would come inside, and Ceese said he would love to, but he was hosting a house party tonight, in just a little while, actually, and would Stephanie and Edgar like to come? He said it was very informal, just families getting together and some musicians playing. Edgar's mother said she loved music, which was true, she did, so it was settled. Then Ceese gave Edgar's mother a huge hug on the drawbridge in the darkness of the evening and said, "You're going to fit right in here!" And when he took a step backward, Edgar wondered if he was going to fall off the drawbridge, but he didn't. He turned gracefully and walked back to his own house just down the street.

Edgar's mother stood in the doorway, glowing dangerously.

"Do you think she's beautiful?" Edgar asked.

"Who?"

"Victoria! She was the one who made dinner!"

She gave him her puzzled look then, as if she had no idea what he was really talking about. She found the switch for the light by the front door and turned it on. It was snowing just a bit, and the darkening sky seemed to vibrate silently with its own blackness. Or, not really blackness, a sort of gray that made Edgar think there were miles and miles of snow in the sky above them, waiting to come down.

They didn't wait to reheat the moose chili, which was a little warm still anyway. They sat at the kitchen table and wolfed it down, maybe the way a wolf would eat a moose it has hunted. It was hard to say what was different about the meat, but it was delicious. Edgar imagined being a wolf fighting against a huge moose. Then he remembered that wolves run in packs. He wouldn't have to hunt a moose all by himself.

"This is so good," his mother murmured.

The plates were very white with a blue pattern around the edge. Edgar washed the moose chili down with big gulps of water and decided he would rather be the moose, be bigger than everything and independent, and if that meant fighting off wolves, then that's what his antlers would be for. Ceese was more like a moose than a wolf, he thought—big and brash and okay all on his own.

Except Ceese wasn't on his own. He had Victoria, who cooked like this and probably reminded him of things like telling Edgar and his mother to keep the water drip-drip-dripping.

(*Victoria must be beautiful*, Edgar thought. *She must be kind and good to talk to, like Caroline.*)

"I told you this was going to work out," his mother said. "I told you people would be friendly here."

She *had* said that, it was true. But she had said many

other things too: that Roger was driving her crazy; that she would never, ever work as a waitress or bartender again; that she would not drink again either. By "drink" she had meant alcohol, which was what everyone drank in restaurants and at parties. Even in Dawson?

They would find out.

"I hope I'll get to meet Benjamin at the party," Edgar said.

"There will be lots of people at the party," Edgar's mother said in the distracted way that she had sometimes, apparently forgetting again that Benjamin was a dog.

PARTY

BEFORE THEY COULD GO TO THE PARTY, Edgar's mother insisted on cleaning up, which she did— to the last drop of dishwater, and Edgar had to dry everything and put it all away exactly where they had found it, in every right cupboard and drawer and slot. Then his mother took forever unpacking and going through her clothes, the way she did when she was serious, when it was not just a party at all that she was going to but something else.

She was getting ready in case she met the next Roger, whoever he was going to be.

Not Ceese, not Ceese, not Ceese, Edgar thought. He was a nice enough man, but he already had a Victoria, and there could be a great deal of trouble if his mother forgot that, or didn't take care.

Finally his mother was ready. She was wearing old clothes, but they didn't look old. Her blue jeans fit tight to her body, and she wore a soft black silk shirt that wouldn't be any warmer than a T-shirt, and a red scarf that disappeared into her shirt, and her hair swooped back, and she had done her face so that everyone would look at her, the men especially.

Probably there would be men at the party.

"What?" she said when she saw his expression. "Have I got something on my teeth?" She rubbed her front teeth with her fingers, then disappeared into the bathroom again to have a look.

Her teeth were perfect.

"We'll just stay for a little bit to meet the neighbors," she said.

"And I can meet Benjamin," Edgar said.

It was a shame they had to put on their winter jackets. Edgar had taken his off when he was drying the dishes, since the house had begun to warm up, and his mother looked ordinary again when she wrapped herself in her old coat. But she would not stay ordinary for long, and he doubted this was going to be a short visit either. They had come so far, and his mother especially had slept through the afternoon.

They stepped out of the new house and leaned into the

darkness and the cold. His mother said to him, "Thank you, Edgar, for being my calm little man."

They kept walking.

"I know how much you do for me," she said. "You have to believe me that I'm trying to provide a stable environment for you."

It wasn't far to Caroline's house.

"I know there's a lot of normal stuff I can't give you, but at least every day is interesting," she said.

Edgar knew he was supposed to say something, or even to give her a hug and be all mushy. *"I just want to meet Benjamin!"* he almost blurted. But that might be the wrong thing. She might think he liked a dog he'd never met better than a mother he knew too well. So he just kept walking, as if he hadn't heard.

At the door: a chaos of boots, so many that Edgar and his mother could hardly walk in without treading on someone's footwear. Edgar pulled his off, then stepped into a cold puddle of slush, soaking his left foot, before he got clear into the crowded living room, where everyone was squished on sofas and chairs, holding drinks, talking at once. Where were Benjamin and Caroline? Edgar saw only people, adults, most of them wearing blue jeans and sweaters. Ceese pulled Edgar and his mother inside and began to introduce them to too many people to keep track of: a tall, tall man named William; another thick man named Zack, with a twisted bush of a beard; a woman with her hair in a scarf whose name was either Zoey or Chloe; a quiet man with a curved nose who looked at Edgar too long before tilting his beer at him and nodding his head. Ross?

It was hard for anyone to see Edgar while his mother was in the room anyway, so Edgar pulled back his ears and cheeks and disappeared. This house seemed to be made of actual logs—big, rounded ones stripped of their bark and piled on top of one another like in pioneer days.

Edgar wandered invisibly among the press of adult bodies into the kitchen. The house was on the same side of the street as their new borrowed house, so part of it was on the side of a hill as well. He peered out the kitchen window at the lights of the town below. Was there a shed out back where Benjamin lived?

In the kitchen a tall woman with a beautifully hooked nose and brown hair tied behind her back was pouring drinks at the counter. Someone said something, and her eyes shone, and then she turned and spied Edgar even though he was pulling his cheeks back. Immediately she said, "Are you Edgar?" and he knew she was Victoria because of the warmth coming from her. What could he say? He knew she was not Caroline's mother, and yet there was the same sense to her as he got from Caroline, the same feeling—of how he just wanted to look at her and be near.

"You must be exhausted! I know you've had a lot of travel in the last few days."

Edgar couldn't think of what to say.

"I think Caroline is downstairs with Benjamin. Shall I take you down? Would you like some ginger ale first?"

The ginger ale was cold and tickled his nose. He liked to look at Victoria's thick hair and the softness of her skin. She smelled, too, of lemon or something, and wood smoke.

She brought him down to the lower level of the house, to one of the back bedrooms, where Benjamin was a huge black form lying on a blanket beside a bed. He did not wake up when Victoria opened the door, but he did raise his large head when Edgar knelt beside him and stroked the long hair on his neck.

"He looks like a bear," Edgar said.

"He's a great big sissy," Victoria said. "He will stay there all day if you pet him like that, and slobber all over you. He's fourteen."

Edgar had never cared for a dog before, but he knew that fourteen was old. Benjamin's tongue hung out, pink in the gray light. Drool dripped down the great black edges of his lips.

"Hello, Benjamin," Edgar said. "I have come a long way to meet you."

Now that they had met, finally, Edgar felt like this was exactly how it was supposed to be.

"I'll see if I can find Caroline," Victoria said. Almost immediately music started upstairs, and Victoria said he should go up again if he wanted a good seat. But Edgar was happy where he was, stroking Benjamin's unruly fur, so she left him there. The music sounded like a lot of instruments, maybe fiddles and guitars. Sometimes people sang, and sometimes, from the noise on the floor above, it sounded like they were dancing, too.

Benjamin held his head up for a long time while Edgar scratched between his floppy ears. His head seemed about as big as Edgar's chest, and it took two hands to really scratch well.

It was safe here, and dark, and quiet except for the music above. Sometimes he heard his mother's laughter rising over everything else, and once he heard her exclaim, "Not on your life!" but he didn't know what she was talking about.

Benjamin smelled pretty doggy, and it didn't take long for Edgar's ginger ale to smell doggy too. He moved it away from Benjamin on the floor to a spot where, he hoped, he would not kick it over in the darkness. He said to the dog, "Do you know where Toronto is?"

Benjamin leaned, leaned against him.

"From here you would have to travel for two days at least. Probably more. It's on the other side of the clouds and the mountains. Some people there, they have subway eyes. Do you know what those are?"

He turned his eyes ice cold and looked away from the dog at the grayness on the floor.

"Some of the schools are all right, and some are like prisons. You sit very still so you don't get in trouble."

Benjamin said to him, "What's school? What's prison? What's subway?"

He asked without moving his lips much. Edgar had never spoken to a dog before, and yet somehow he wasn't surprised at understanding. Hadn't he known, ever since first hearing Benjamin's name, that they would have this unusual connection?

"All those are things in Toronto," Edgar said. "Maybe the only one of them here is school. Where the kids go."

Benjamin farted. The cloud of stink filled the room, and Edgar waved his hand in front of his nose.

He heard a noise. "Edgar, are you here?" Caroline asked.

"We both are!" Edgar said.

"Oh, God, Benjamin? We've got to get you outside!" Caroline flipped on a light, and Benjamin half sat up, awkwardly, dislodging Edgar. Caroline said, "Or is that you who farted?"

"No." Edgar picked up his ginger ale so he wouldn't forget it.

"So I was just listening to your mother upstairs," Caroline said. "Were you running away from a murderer or something?"

What was she talking about? Roger wasn't very nice sometimes, but he wasn't a murderer.

"He's not going to follow you here, is he? Because I have a rifle if he does."

"You have a rifle?"

"It's just a .22, for hunting. You wouldn't use it for a bear. It'll stop a man, though."

"He won't be coming here," Edgar said. "And he isn't a murderer. I don't think he has a gun. He had a camera, which he gave to me."

"I saw Jason Crumley trip you at the airport because of it. Remember?" She pinched him a little. "Are you some kind of boy genius or something?"

"Did my mom say that?" Edgar asked.

"She said it to your face back at the airport. I heard it!" Caroline said. "And then she made fun of you."

Edgar rubbed Benjamin through his thick fur, and he felt his face baking again. "I took some tests a couple of times," he said quietly. "Didn't mean anything."

"I hate it when parents are awful like that," she said. "Just now upstairs your mother said that in Toronto there were bodies on the streets."

What could she have meant? He said, "Sometimes you see homeless people downtown." He thought of them sitting on cardboard boxes, their skin red where it pressed against the cold. They could be frightening.

"But they're not, like—dead corpses," Caroline prompted.

"No, not dead," Edgar said. Then he added: "On the news sometimes, there are shootings."

Caroline was leaning close to him, and she couldn't help it, she was stroking Benjamin too. "Your mother shouldn't come to a new place and just start lying like this," she said.

Edgar stayed quiet. Now Benjamin couldn't seem to decide whether he wanted to lie down or go for a walk. Even so, just halfway up, he was enormous.

"And," Caroline said, "you didn't answer my question."

"About the corpses?"

"What you're running away from."

From Roger, obviously. But she didn't know Roger, so

how would she understand? In a way, though, they were running from the corpses, too, from the homeless people on the cardboard. From his mother's fear of how quickly she and Edgar might find themselves exactly there, with the same red blisters on their skin.

It was all too much to say right then.

So Edgar said instead, "Does Benjamin need a walk?"

It didn't take very much for Edgar and Caroline to leave the party, even though it was late and dark and cold outside. The adults were still singing and dancing. Edgar saw his mother in the living room on an old couch sitting quite close to Ceese, and she had a beer in her hand. When she saw Edgar with Caroline and Benjamin, she called out, "Oh, Edgar, is that the dog? God, he's huge!"

"He's a Newfoundland," Caroline said. "Pretty stinky these days. We won't be long."

Benjamin sniffed, sniffed in the general direction of the party, a roomful of people who might pet him if he stopped long enough. Caroline pulled at his collar.

Victoria was on the other side of the room talking to the tall, tall man, William, but she was looking at Edgar's mother and at Ceese. Edgar glanced back at his mother, but she wasn't noticing Victoria, or she was pretending not to notice.

Edgar swallowed. He couldn't think of what to say. Then Benjamin started forward after all.

There wasn't a drawbridge to this house. The road was slippery with ice and snow, and Benjamin walked like he was afraid to fall. They had a leash for him, though Caroline had said they would not need it much. Benjamin didn't run anymore.

"What grade are you in?" Caroline asked.

Edgar kicked a chunk of ice, and it spun down the road until it hit something and broke into several pieces.

"You *did* go to school in Toronto, didn't you?" she said.

Benjamin farted with every step. It was good that they were outside in a lot of air.

"Sometimes," Edgar said.

"How could you only go to school sometimes?"

It was a complicated question. Sometimes Edgar stayed home and read books, and sometimes he and his mother were moving and didn't know how long they would be able to stay on someone's couch or in their basement, and it would have been a bother starting in a new school when they really weren't sure how long the arrangement would last.

Sometimes Edgar went to school and pulled his cheeks back and the people didn't really know he was there.

"What's school like here?" Edgar asked.

Caroline said, "It's just school. Probably like anywhere!"

Benjamin took a big poop on the road in front of a very old log cabin that Caroline said used to belong to Robert Service, a poet who got rich writing about the Klondike. But the cabin did not look like a rich man's house at all. There was still bark on the logs and the house itself seemed tiny and dark and cold. It did have a big veranda, though. Caroline worked a plastic bag so that she could pick up the poop without getting her hand dirty. Then she tied it closed and handed it to Edgar.

Edgar spied another old log cabin down the road, and Caroline said it had belonged to Jack London.

"Really?" Edgar said. Jack London had written the story Edgar had been thinking about on the road from the airport, about the freezing man and the dog and the fire.

"What people say about Jack London around here," Caroline told him, "is that he got stranded on an island upriver when winter came on. He holed up in a cabin, probably a lot like that one, with a whole bunch of others, and all they could do for months was tell stories. That was his gold rush! He went back to San Francisco and wrote them up."

Edgar asked, and Caroline said she did know the story of the freezing man, she'd read it in school. Edgar spat, but it didn't crackle and freeze in midair.

"Pretty balmy tonight, actually," Caroline said, but she spat too.

The sky was a brilliant darkness above them. Caroline turned them off the street and up the hill farther into the woods along a trail Edgar would not have noticed on his own. In just a couple of minutes it felt like they were far away from everything, were in the middle of frozen trees. Benjamin was happier with the footing, and he seemed to like stopping and sniffing.

Caroline said, "Listen. Just listen."

So they stood still. Benjamin snorted and huffed, and Edgar felt he could even hear the dog's drool dripping onto the snow and freezing there, slowly. He could hear his own breathing, because he was puffing still from climbing the hill. As he listened further, he could hear the sounds of the party, the music, laughter, a song about a man riding a motorcycle. And, even farther away, he could hear the sound of an engine, a car or truck coughing into life.

A dog howled; Benjamin pricked up his ears. It was a lonely sound from far away. Other dogs began to bark, and the barking echoed off the hills, a chorus of dogs, some now howling. Benjamin stayed quiet, but he was listening.

"Dog radio," Caroline said. "Who knows what they're talking about?"

It was cold as they stood on the trail, their breath coming out in clouds. Was this balmy? Edgar felt like his cheeks were becoming thicker, maybe even freezing. But it didn't hurt. There was no wind at all. The plastic bag in his hand, Benjamin's poop, was solidifying. He heard a clanking sound from far away, and then he could hear someone chopping wood.

She was fine to just stand still, this girl Caroline. She didn't need to be talking all the time. And neither did Benjamin. But there would be things to say. He and Benjamin, and maybe even Caroline, were going to be great, great friends.

Finally Caroline said, "So, who's your father?"

More chopping in the distance. Edgar imagined a big man in a lumberjack shirt with one of those double-edged axes from old pictures. But that couldn't be right. An axe like that would've been for cutting down a tree, not splitting wood for the fire.

"Don't answer that if you don't want to," Caroline said finally. "Lots of families here don't follow any traditional pattern. As you see from my family!" She shrugged. Benjamin sniffed at Edgar's boot for a moment, then nuzzled him gently, but it was almost enough to knock Edgar back a step.

"He likes you," Caroline said.

"My father is a musician somewhere," Edgar said. "I don't know him. He and my mom were just friends. She has a lot of those."

"Victoria's a singer!" Caroline said. "And my dad is a killer drummer. You should hear them together."

"My mother is a singer too," Edgar said. "Sometimes."

"Yeah, well, Victoria's *really* good!" Caroline said.

Yes, he could imagine it. He could imagine it all coming to a great deal of trouble.

They listened some more. Then they headed back down the trail.

If anything, there were more boots in the hall than before. The party was not winding down. Edgar's mother had moved to the kitchen. She had her back to the counter, was holding a nearly empty glass of red wine now, and a different man—younger than her possibly, but with very little hair on his head—was pressing close while they talked.

Edgar and Caroline brought Benjamin back down to the bedroom on the lower level. Edgar put the frozen plastic bag with Benjamin's poop into a special container with a lid that closed tight.

"Why would your mother say her boyfriend tried to kill her in Toronto?" Caroline asked. She was lying back on the bed with her legs crossed at the ankles. She had opened a window to clear out the smell of Benjamin's farts, and cold air was pouring in.

Edgar set his eyes to somewhere above her head. A steering-wheel lamp burned dully.

"Are you sure he didn't have a knife?" Caroline said. "He wasn't screaming?"

What had his mother said to these people?

"Roger did get loud when he was angry," Edgar said.

"But you left, like, in the middle of the night. When he was drunk on the floor?"

His mother had told them what she needed to say to get a free house for a while, he realized.

"We did leave quickly," Edgar said.

"But you don't think he'll come here? What if he finds out where you are?" Her eyes had a gleamy look, like she wanted it all to be true. She wanted to see Roger with his knife dripping blood.

"I should have brought my camera," Edgar said. He wanted to take Caroline's picture right now, lying back, with her hands over her head, hoping for gore.

She had a sneaky smile that he liked to look at.

"If the murderer does come here," she said, "we'll sic Benjamin on him, won't we?" She reached down to pet the dog's long body. Benjamin did not respond. He had fallen asleep as soon as he'd settled on the smelly rug.

"There are places I can take you if he comes back," Caroline said. "I know exactly where to hide out."

Edgar imagined Roger, right here in the house, sitting in the living room, crying.

"We could start in the back room of the old brothel," she said. "And there's an attic in the commissioner's residence. I know the way in. If the guy is really dangerous, we'll head to the Paddlewheel Graveyard, set up a tent." She just seemed to like to talk about it. "You'd like it—it's where they dumped all the old wooden paddle-wheelers when the road finally got built. It's like a boat cemetery. I'll bring my rifle."

Someone was playing music again above their heads. Edgar thought about going back upstairs and asking his mother for the key, returning to his new bedroom in his new house on his own. But he would have to stand in front of whatever man she was talking to now so closely. And it was warm and dark here with Caroline and Benjamin. Despite what she was saying, he enjoyed the sound of her voice. If she needed to keep talking now, that was fine. He lay on the bed beside her and crossed his ankles, and felt the soft embrace of the pillow.

DREAM

EDGAR TRIED TO STAY AWAKE IN HIS DREAM for a while, just to look around. It was one thing to be here in Dawson, so far from everything else, but he also knew that part of everything else was still in his head and he could go visit it. He thought about the glass house in the park in Toronto, where the green plants were and it was warm and fragrant even in the winter. He would go sometimes just to sit and smell and pretend that he was in the jungle even though there was snow outside. He had a favorite bench. He went there now in his dream. He sat down and folded his hands and looked at the tall tropical plant with the big leaves. Probably it was a tree. There were no flowers, but the whole room smelled like flowers anyway, and though it felt like a jungle, there were no panthers. You could just breathe.

But it was hard to keep the dream like that. It was one thing to start off a dream the way you wanted it, but he could not keep Roger from stealing into the room. He couldn't keep the door closed. It opened, cold air rushed in, and then the door closed; and he knew from the footsteps that Roger had a knife, and the knife was dripping.

If there had been a panther, then Roger might have used the knife to defend himself.

Edgar felt like he needed to get off the bench and hide, maybe in the smelly bush behind the tropical tree. But his hands were folded, he couldn't move, Roger was getting closer.

Where was his mother?

In Dawson. In the cold. She wasn't going to come in and save him.

Edgar wanted to turn his head, to look at Roger. He had his camera; he would show Roger the pictures. But Edgar's hands were folded. He couldn't seem to be able to make them move. And then Benjamin was there, standing by him, not looking at all at Roger, but somehow Benjamin knew where the knife was, where his teeth would sink best into Roger's wrist.

Edgar woke up cold in the dark. Caroline was sleeping beside him. She had covered herself with a blanket but not him. She twitched when she slept. Her mouth was open;

she made murderer noises when she breathed. Benjamin was on the floor still on his blanket, but he didn't smell as bad as before.

Where was Edgar's mother?

Edgar got up, shivering. He needed to pee; his nose felt cold. The window was still open from before, when they were clearing out the Benjamin stink. It was a big window, but Edgar fought it closed. Neither Benjamin nor Caroline stirred. So Edgar crept in the dark up the stairs looking for the bathroom.

It was strange to be here at this new house that was not even theirs, rather than at the other new house that was not even theirs. All was quiet. His eyes adjusted, and he could see his mother passed out on the sofa in the living room, lying on her front with a blanket over her bottom half, except for her socked feet. No one else was asleep there. A bottle lay on its side on the floor, empty. She was snoring into the sofa cushion.

He found a closed door and pushed it open slightly, but that was a bedroom, people were sleeping there. The next door he tried was the right one. He turned on the light and immediately closed his eyes. It was so bright, he turned it off again.

His mother walked in with her eyes half-closed. "Oh, Jesus!" she said when she saw him. Her hair was the way

it got in the middle of the night. He could imagine raising his camera and framing the whole picture around the
storm of it.

In a bit Edgar found his jacket and boots and waited
in the hallway as his mother stumbled through the darkness toward the door. She knocked into something and
swore, loudly. Edgar couldn't see what it was. But no one
else woke up. A good guard dog would be on top of them,
Edgar thought, but Benjamin was not a good guard dog,
not at his age. He was having dog dreams, no doubt.

Maybe in his dream he was in the greenhouse in Toronto
standing guard there against Roger the so-called murderer.

What time was it? It didn't matter. Edgar's body still
thought he was in Toronto somehow. What was it called?
Jet lag. In Toronto it was already morning. Maybe that's
why he was awake, and his mother, too, despite all the
drink. But here it was black, black. When his mother was
ready, they walked out the door quietly and then down the
road, Eighth Avenue, which was icy and still. It looked
like there was so much more sky here than in Toronto.
But then again, Edgar thought, he did not get to see the
sky in Toronto at this sort of hour very often.

They crossed the moat; his mother went through her
pockets to find the key. It was cold, but if Edgar stayed
very still, the cold forgot about him.

His mother found the key and then dropped it. If it had fallen off the drawbridge where they were standing, then Edgar would've had to somehow climb down and find it in all the snow, in the darkness, at the bottom of the moat (which did not have any water, but still it seemed like a moat) while his mother cursed herself. But it didn't fall any farther than the boards at their feet. Edgar was able to pick it up quickly and open the door.

It didn't feel like home, but it would, he knew. They would be here for a couple of months.

"Did you have a good time?" his mother asked him as they were taking off their coats and boots.

"I should've brought my camera," he said.

"No evidence, no prosecution!" she replied. Edgar looked at her until she explained. "A party like that, people let their hair down. It's probably good you didn't take pictures."

Her hair was down. It was the way it got when the rest of her was becoming unraveled as well. But maybe there was some other reason.

He said, "Did Roger try to hurt you?"

She stopped hanging up her coat. "Oh, baby," she said, and she held him as she did sometimes, when he felt like he was a raft. "Roger is far, far away. That's why we're here. We're never going to have to deal with him again."

She smelled like cigarettes, like wine that has been left in an open bottle.

She held him at arm's length. "He never laid a hand on you, did he?"

Edgar shook his head.

"I didn't think so. Here's the thing about Roger. I didn't feel I could trust him any farther than I could throw him. But he wouldn't let me walk away either. That's why we had to run. That's why we're here."

In the gloom her hair stood out, black against the gray of the walls.

"I'm sorry I drank too much. I know that I do it, and yet, I do it. That will change, I promise. I can tell you that I have a new job. I'm starting tomorrow—tonight— at Lola's. That's a bar. Everybody who was at the party last night goes there. Including the owner, who hired me all because of Ceese. So it was worth it to go."

She hugged him again. He felt her start to cry.

"So tomorrow—today—we're going to have to get you started in the new school," she said.

"We need to buy groceries first," he said quickly.

"Food, yes, then school. First, more sleep. I really can't drink like that anymore," she said, as if she meant it, as if, finally, the way ahead was clear.

RIVER

MORNING. THE GROCERY STORE WAS DOWN the hill, that much Edgar remembered. From the back of the town where they were, the streets either took you toward the river or along it. The hill itself was steep and slippery. His mother's boots had a heel. She had to grab him suddenly when she almost fell, and then for a moment Edgar thought they both would go down, his mother on top of him.

She had a nervous, clutchy strength that shocked through his body.

But he didn't fall, and neither did she. They just crept along like a pair of very old people, or like Benjamin on the trail last night, Edgar thought. Careful and afraid.

They could see their breath, it was so cold. But it wasn't windy. Maybe it rarely was here? In Toronto the winds could cut through your coat like a pair of chilly scissors and make you feel like you were naked in the refrigerator with a big fan blowing.

Now, that would make an interesting picture, Edgar thought.

They reached a flatter part of the road. The streets were wide; nothing else was moving. It was as if the whole town had stayed sensibly in bed. He and his mother were hungry again. She had found some coffee in the cupboard, but it was old, almost worse than having no coffee at all.

On the flatter part his mother did not clutch at him, and she was not in a talking mood. The morning was just the way it was. Gray smoke curled out of some of the house chimneys, and some were dark and still. Maybe no one was in those houses. Maybe their owners had headed south like the Summerhills?

Two ravens—together they looked almost as big as Edgar—flew overhead and perched on the telephone pole to bark and mutter at them. Were they the same couple he had seen on the walk in from the airport?

Edgar saw what they were looking at: on the hill far above the town, partly buried in snow but partly just black, open rock, it looked like some huge hand had scooped away half the mountain. Edgar opened his jacket and took out his camera. He had to pull his mittens off to free the lens, and he had to stop walking to peer through the viewfinder.

His mother kept on. She was talking to herself.

Edgar zoomed in and out. The scooped-out part looked much smaller in the viewfinder, where the giant had torn away the rock. Edgar turned his camera sideways, then shifted it back again before clicking the picture.

"Edgar!" His mother's lips were pale. She had tied her hair behind her in a big knot and her eyes were as cold as the air.

"What is it?" He was looking still at the gash in the mountain.

"We have to get some bloody breakfast!"

Now he was just trying to keep up with her. When she had to, she could hurry ferociously. Of course this was not Toronto, so he didn't have to be careful about the traffic. He wasn't going to disappear in a subway crowd. Even as she pulled away from him, he could see her.

Were they going to buy breakfast again at the Eldorado? There it was, a big gray building with purple trim surrounded by wooden sidewalks. A red pickup truck was parked nearby. Not Ceese's—that was silver. A man in tired clothes, one of the men from breakfast yesterday, stood on the veranda of the hotel smoking a cigarette and staring at them as they approached.

Staring again at Edgar's mother.

"Morning," he said when they were close enough. As if announcing the bare fact of it.

"Yes, hello," his mother said.

They walked past breakfast. The grocery store was closer to the water, Edgar remembered from Ceese and Caroline's directions. At the front of the town.

The General Store. It was opposite the exhausted building Edgar also remembered from yesterday, with peeling yellow paint and boarded-up windows, that looked like it had been left there—abandoned?—like a ship no longer in the water. In fact there was a big ship quite close to it. How had he missed it yesterday? A white boat with snow on it, old-fashioned, with a contraption at the back, maybe a paddle wheel?

Was this the Paddlewheel Graveyard that Caroline had mentioned? It didn't look like a place to hide from a murdering Roger, or anybody, for long. True, both the peeling building and the abandoned ship looked empty. There would be places to creep around in, disappear. But the General Store—and other buildings—were right here. Everybody would see you when you showed your face.

Edgar took out his camera again. His mother had gone into the store. The air was cold on his fingers, but at least the day was bright, perfect for pictures. He wanted the peeling building and the old ship both to fit into one frame. He could see them at the same time with his eyes, but he could not see them both with the camera . . . with the camera's eye. So he took pictures of one after the other, and he wondered for a moment, if you were an ant, or some other small insect, what would the giant world look like all around you? How much of it would you see?

Flies had many eyes. Maybe they saw many worlds?

Where was his lens cap? In his pocket. He didn't want to leave the camera on for long. The battery would run out in the cold. That was another thing Roger had told him. Did that mean, Edgar wondered now, that Roger had known that he and his mother were traveling farther and farther into winter? Or had he just been talking about Toronto cold when he'd talked about the battery? It was still chilly there, but not with snow lining the streets, not like this.

Edgar climbed the stairs and opened the door. The store was small, not a Super anything. Anyone pushing a cart around was going to bump into other people.

His mother had a cart, and she was bending down to look at tomatoes. It was hard to see what was so interesting about them. They looked small, pale, hard. Maybe not something to eat right away, but they would ripen on a windowsill or kitchen counter. His mother said to him, "Look how expensive these are!"

Of course she would know if six dollars was expensive or not for food you wouldn't be able to eat right away even though you were hungry.

"Do you want me to get anything?" he asked. Sometimes in a grocery store she sent him up the aisle for oatmeal, for biscuits, and other things.

"I have to keep track of how much we're racking up," she said. She put the tomatoes into the cart despite the six dollars. "But I will be working tonight. That's already good luck."

It *was* lucky, Edgar could see that. He was lucky to have a camera. They were lucky to have a house for free, to be here in the store shopping for food even if it was too expensive.

They were hungry, but soon they would be back in the kitchen making breakfast.

"Oh my God, the cheese!" his mother said. She had pulled a big white chunk of it off the cold shelf. "Fifty-five dollars!"

She said the words, but in her eyes she was laughing, it was not a disaster. They were here now. The tomatoes would ripen. They didn't have to buy cheese.

His mother would have her real coffee soon.

— — —

"Let's have a look at the river!" his mother said when they were outside, carrying the grocery bags. Even though the river was just across the street, they couldn't see it. A big mound ran all along, hiding it from view. What was it called? A dike? They crossed Front Street—no traffic anywhere, even though this was as downtown as Dawson got. Edgar could see that already. Then they walked past the flaking old yellow building. Maybe when it had been new, it had looked like gold, Edgar thought.

"This used to be the bank," his mother said. "That's where Robert Service worked. The poet."

Edgar remembered the old log hut from the night before, and his mother recited: "There are strange things done in the midnight sun / By the men who moil for gold . . ."

She ran out after a couple of lines. "We'll look it up!" she said, too brightly. Her face seemed to say it was all good, good, maybe too good. Everything was going to be gold.

They climbed the bank of the mound, the dike, whatever it was. The white flatness of the snow and ice was hedged in by the steep slopes of snow- and tree-clad hills across the way. Edgar took picture after picture up and down the river. To his right he saw the orange pylon— actually a tall wooden orange pole braced on the ice—

with the wire leading to shore. That was how they would know when the ice started to move, he remembered. There was, quite close to it, a sliver of black, open water, before the river turned. So maybe it wouldn't be too long? And—did they lose the pylon every year, with it sinking into the river? Or would it float?

Islands in the distance. To his left he could see where some other white flat expanse met this one—the Klondike meeting the Yukon. Which was the big river? He thought of the squiggles on the old map, the one that was probably out of date, the one that said West Dawson and Moosehide and other places were abandoned. The Yukon was the big river.

Even if the map was out of date, maybe rivers don't change that much?

"Let's just go down. I think there's a trail," his mother said.

Edgar was carrying two plastic bags of groceries, including the eggs, so he had to be careful. If he slipped, everything would be ruined. But the path was not too difficult. Even his mother made it to the bottom safely. She immediately started walking along a smoothed-out part. "It's a snowmobile trail," she said, sounding proud of herself for knowing.

The snow was packed, even, easy to walk on. When

Edgar turned back to look at the town, it was gone. All he saw was the high slope of the riverbank and the wall. They were standing in the middle of wilderness surrounded by hills, snow, sky, ice, earth.

It was quiet, too, except for the crunching of their boots. Sometimes they stepped on hard snow and sometimes on bluish ice that made a hollow, musical sound. There was no wind. The sky was lightening into a bright, bright blue.

Their breathing. The musical footsteps. The rustle of the grocery bags as they rubbed sometimes against their pants.

"This is so beautiful!" his mother said.

It was. In a few minutes they were that much closer to a dramatic spot where the hills seemed to plunge down into the meeting place of the rivers. So Edgar took out his camera again and captured picture after picture. Then his mother paused to look into a deep crack in the ice. *You could lose your foot down there if you stepped the wrong way,* Edgar thought.

"Isn't this gorgeous?" his mother said again.

"Be careful!" Edgar said. He was thinking again of that story, of the man falling through the ice.

"Oh, don't you worry!" his mother said in her sunny voice, her best one.

She had forgotten about breakfast. Where were they walking, anyway? Edgar had only a vague sense now of where their house was. Back there, up the bank, on the other side of the town that they seemed to be walking away from.

"Let's keep going. Let's see where this leads," his mother said. He didn't say that he was hungry again. It could wait. School could wait too.

This was all good right now.

A silver truck crossed the river. It was driving on the ice and stopped just as Edgar and his mother came to it. Ceese again, still in his jean jacket. He looked delighted to see them.

"Got some groceries, then?" he said.

And Edgar's mother cracked open in front of him. She went on and on in her way about how spectacular the scenery was, how friendly everyone had been, especially at the party last night. She thanked him for "everything you did" to get her the job at Lola's, starting tonight.

What, what had he done? Edgar wondered.

Ceese had his door open with the engine running while Edgar and his mother stood below him, on the ice. He seemed to be parked in the middle of the road—an orange sign called it an ice bridge—but no one else was on it, so why not?

"How about you, young Edgar? How are you enjoying Dawson?" Ceese asked.

It was hard not to smile at him.

"What's your favorite thing about our town so far?" Ceese pressed.

Edgar's mother was looking, looking, so Edgar had to say something. "Benjamin," he whispered finally, but he meant Caroline, too.

Ceese drove them back to their new house. Along the way he explained—since Edgar had asked—that the gouge in the mountain outside of town was called the Moosehide Slide, which had happened, as far as any-one knew, thousands of years ago when tons of rock had suddenly fallen off the face. "Some people think there's an Indian village—we say 'First Nations' now—buried beneath the rock, but that's just a story," he said. "And it has nothing to do with mining. Do you see how it looks like a big moosehide stretched out for drying?"

It did look something like that, although it was hard to really see it clearly as they were driving.

"'Moosehide' is also the name of the summer vil-lage downriver where the local Hän people, the Tr'ondëk Hwëch'in"—Ceese's lips slipped over the tribal names quickly—"moved to when the gold rushers really started swarming the area. Chief Isaac got on with everyone, even the whites. But the miners were kind of like mosquitoes. What can you do when there are so many of them swarming? Sometimes you just get out of the way and wait for the madness to pass."

Ceese kept talking, almost as if he needed to do something to fill in any possible silence. All the time his eyes were memorizing Edgar's mother, who seemed in turn to be memorizing him right back again. Ceese went from Chief Isaac to the ice bridge without even a pause for breath. He said that the route for the bridge was about a quarter mile upstream this year from where it usually got built because the ice was too thin at the normal crossing point. "It's been a milder winter. We've had a whole spate of those!" he said.

As he drove, he turned his head constantly to look at Edgar's mother, and sometimes also at Edgar. A few times a vehicle passed by, but mostly the streets were quiet. He didn't seem to have to worry about hitting anything.

"What's on the other side of the river?" Edgar's mother asked.

"The Top of the World Highway. It goes all the way to Alaska," Ceese said. "You'll see the tourists coming over in May and June. Closer to home, of course, there's West Dawson. That's where the real eccentrics of Dawson live. It's off the grid, no electricity except what you make yourself." He paused. "Victoria, who you met last night, lives in West Dawson with her dogs."

Edgar's mother smiled and said that she was sorry she hadn't talked to Victoria more at the party.

She was smiling, smiling, and her face was set like porcelain. *Victoria, Victoria, who cares about her?* she seemed to be saying. Everything was good this morning, the sun was pouring down, nothing could be sour or cruel.

And Edgar thought about how just a name, Chief Isaac, conjured up someone wise and strong. Someone who knew enough to move down the river to Moosehide—the village, not the slide—when a bad-luck cloud of mosquitoes came swarming.

At least they had a place to go, he thought.

Edgar's mother convinced Ceese to stay, since he had bought them breakfast the day before. She made a mushroom omelette, using powdered cheese that she found in the cupboard and at least half the eggs they had bought. Edgar was in charge of the toast. The butter was hard, so he microwaved it for a few seconds, enough to soften it without melting.

Ceese talked about the youngest of Victoria's dogs, Rupert, who'd nearly been lured out of his doghouse to join the wolves pretending to play outside his pen. "I heard something in the night," Ceese said, "and wandered out, and there they all were, four hungry wolves trying not to lick their chops too loud, and young Rupert sticking his nose out his doghouse door, whining like he really wanted to roll around with them and he couldn't quite remember why he shouldn't."

His mother laughed; she turned into a field of daisies. Edgar remembered driving past just such a field. He had been in the back of Roger's car, white sunshine waving in the breeze.

His mother heaped eggs onto Ceese's plate. She squeezed his big shoulder when she told him how wonderful he had been yesterday, picking them up on the frozen highway and buying them breakfast and everything.

"I was the one late to come get you!" Ceese said. "Anyway, that's the north. The land is hard enough if we aren't looking out for one another." His face creased, smiling. Edgar's mother let her hand linger on the back of his neck.

The coffee was brewing. The whole kitchen smelled of good food. Ceese's eyes followed Edgar's mother from stove to fridge to table to the garbage can, where she scraped the eggshells and orange peelings.

"How's the sausage?" she asked. The meat was gray, tough, not pork or beef, which they ate in Toronto, but something different. Elk?

"I've got some moose meat sausages in my freezer I'll bring over next time," Ceese said. "Some of the store pickings by now are pretty slim."

"I could use some slimming myself," Edgar's mother said. She was in her blue jeans and didn't even have a sweater on. She seemed to be hot, doing all the cooking.

"You look perfect to me," Ceese said, taking a big bite of the omelette. He couldn't pull his eyes from her.

Edgar's mother turned back to the frying pan and tried to hide her smile.

Edgar thought: *He has a lady friend. Victoria.*
We have met her!

His mother knew and Ceese knew, and yet the sausages were sizzling, the eggs were fluffy on the plate.

She couldn't keep from touching him on the shoulder whenever she passed by.

"I have such a good feeling about this place," she said dreamily when she sat down at last to have her coffee. Her fingers twitched on the cup. She probably needed to go outside and have a smoke, but she would wait. She didn't want Ceese to see her lighting up.

Edgar ate his eggs and watched them both.

He thought: *She never goes long without a Roger.*

And: *When she finds him, she gets him. One way or the other.*

Edgar scraped his plate and said, "Is Caroline home?"

His mother and Ceese did not even hear, they were so locked on each other.

And the air . . . the air started to lock up too. What was it? Edgar's jaw felt cruel and his lungs stiffened, his throat dried. It wasn't fair, any of it. Words shrank, he had to move. The world burned now, all of it unbearably from inside his own skin. He had to move, he had to go. They didn't notice him disappearing at all.

DOG

THEY WERE THE FIRE, CEESE AND EDGAR'S mother. Once they started, look out! They could take a whole house down in just a few hours. Edgar had watched just such a fire in the Toronto neighborhood where they had lived before Roger, how a half dozen screaming trucks had arrived at once and sprayed water into the burning building but there was nothing anyone could do. The flames took hold, the stench rose, smoke poured out of every window.

Ceese and his mother, his mother and Ceese—what should he do? Breathe first, breathe. Get his own jaw back. He could tell Caroline and Victoria. They might be able to unhypnotize Ceese, if that was possible. Before something happened . . .

Sometimes people could be hypnotized, or they fell

into a sort of dream even when they were wide awake.
Especially Edgar's mother, especially about men. As
she was right now. Edgar pulled on his boots and coat,
plunged out the door. She would know, and yet somehow she wouldn't. Later on she would sort of wake up
from the dream, which was not really a dream, and
she would say to herself, "Where's Edgar?" Or even:
"What was I thinking? Why did I do that?" And there
would be a moment of panic, as happens sometimes in
a dream, too.

Eighth Avenue sat in shadows, the road icy. Still, he
didn't have to walk far. He knocked on Caroline's door
and waited, blowing his breath out hard in clouds. How
could it be so cold outside and on-fire beneath his skin?

But no one came to the door. Was it a school day for
Caroline? Edgar and his mother had been supposed to
check out school for him after groceries and breakfast.
Edgar was in no hurry for that plan anyway, and now
his mother was hypnotized. What day was it, anyway?
They'd been on the run for more than a week; he'd lost
track. And he thought: *Of course Victoria is not here either.
She lives in West Dawson.* Probably Ceese had been driving back from there this morning when he'd stopped on
the ice road to pick up Edgar and his mother.

If Caroline was in school, then maybe she wouldn't

mind if Edgar looked in on Benjamin. Edgar was supposed to be taking care of him, after all. So Edgar tramped
in the snow down the hill to the back of the house, where
the lower bedroom was. The window was grimy from
winter, but Edgar thought he could see Benjamin's big
black form on the rug between the bed and the wall. The
back door opened easily.

"Hello! Hello, it's Edgar!" he called. There, his
throat was back. Benjamin made a snuffling, getting-
up noise, then came around to sniff at Edgar. His leash
was hanging on the wall by the door—red, chewed,
easy to reach—so Edgar clipped it onto the dog's thick
collar just to be safe and led Benjamin into the backyard, which got a bit of sunshine, anyway. "How are you
today?" Edgar patted Benjamin's shaggy head. "Do you
want to go for a walk?"

Edgar only noticed that his heart had been hammer-
ing when it started to slow on its own.

I like Ceese, Edgar thought. *But he already has a Victoria.*

It was easier for Benjamin to walk a little farther down
the hill to the lane behind the house than to try climbing
the icy slope back up to Eighth Avenue. They followed the
lane a short distance in behind the new borrowed house.
In the kitchen window Edgar's mother and Ceese were at
the table, still talking. Ceese was saying something, prob-

ably telling a story, his hand resting not far from Edgar's mother's elbow.

It was happening. Edgar knew the signs, the inside sickening started to come back. He would have to tell Victoria or Caroline, whoever he saw first.

But what could they do, except start to feel terrible themselves? Edgar's mother was a storm on a big lake. When she knew where she wanted to go . . . And when it all came out, there would be tears then, and shouting, and a lot of drinking, fists punching walls (now *that*, Roger could do), and angry phone calls, and probably another uprooting, Edgar and his mother packing their bags in the middle of the night. Where do you go when you're practically at the North Pole anyway? Where *would* they go?

Edgar and Benjamin reached a cross street that had been sanded, so Benjamin was able to climb despite the ice, as long as they went slowly. Edgar let him sniff, his floppy red tongue hanging out like a loose smile. They took the trail into the woods. It was the same path they had been on the night before, but it looked completely different in the daylight. Benjamin stopped to sniff something else interesting in the snow.

"Have Ceese and Victoria been together a long time?" Edgar asked. He couldn't stop thinking about everything that was going to go wrong.

Benjamin sniffed, sniffed.

"My mother is going to break them up. She wants him for herself," Edgar said. "I don't know why she acts this way."

Benjamin raised his head. "Soon this whole hillside will stink of bears. It's the melt. Makes everyone crazy."

Edgar said, "I like Victoria. She and Caroline are going to be very sad soon."

Benjamin huffed. "No bears yet, though. They still lie cold, round about now."

"Should I tell someone?" Edgar asked. Benjamin was so old, he might know what to do.

Benjamin snuffed and snorted. "No bears yet," he said again.

"But what about my mother and Ceese?" Edgar said.

From Benjamin's lips a line of drool slowly stretched to the snow. "Humans," he muttered.

They started walking again along the trail, climbing still. Edgar could feel himself twisting inside, like a wet sheet someone is winding in their hands. Why would his mother choose a Roger, or a Ceese, and take him, as she could, and then grow tired like she always did?

The trail turned. They were still climbing, but now they were on the side of the slope. The town was below them. Edgar could see houses and streets through the bare trees.

They climbed, climbed, and then Benjamin wanted to rest. He stood and panted beside a bench in the woods. Edgar wiped the snow off and sat down.

"Did Caroline take you out this morning?" Edgar asked.

"They all left." Benjamin seemed to be drooling from everywhere, from his black lips, his runny nose, teary eyes. And he was moving so stiffly, he seemed to be in pain.

"Does it hurt?" Edgar asked.

Benjamin laid his huge shaggy head on Edgar's lap so that Edgar could snuggle and pet him with his mitts.

"I'm supposed to be taking care of you from now on," Edgar said. "At least helping, while I'm here."

"You are here," Benjamin said.

"Yes, I am."

The sun rose a little higher; in a moment the bench felt beautifully warm. The snow wasn't melting, but it didn't feel cold, either. Benjamin sniffed in the pockets of Edgar's jacket. "The girl brings treats," he said after a time.

"I'll try to remember!" Edgar said.

Benjamin sniffed and sniffed, smeared his drool down the side of Edgar's jacket.

"How far does the trail go?" Edgar asked. It looked like there were some interesting twists.

But Benjamin turned around and started to pull Edgar back down the hill, toward home.

The house was still empty. Edgar really should have just hung up Benjamin's leash and left. The dog could return to sleep. But Ceese was not here, so probably he was still with Edgar's mother, and Edgar didn't want to walk in on—he didn't even want to think about—what might be happening.

Benjamin pointed to where his dog biscuits were, so Edgar got them from the cupboard. Then when the dog settled down again in his bedroom, Edgar stroked his head and neck and shoulders, and Edgar thought about his old teacher Ms. Nordstrom in her red turtleneck that she wore some days in the winter. She had been on the rowing team in college, and her shoulders looked rounded, strong. Like something you wanted to touch. Sometimes when she was busy at the front with the whiteboard or even if she was just talking, her underarms became dark with the sweat of the moment, and some of the children tittered, but not so loudly that she might hear. Edgar liked the darkness, just as he liked the shape of her shoulders and the way that she moved, like her whole body was pulling in one direction.

Was that a way to love someone? he wondered. To

think about shoulders and sweat stains and how a body moved from the desk to the bookshelves? Was it the same as sitting quietly and stroking the fur of an old, smelly dog who purred and grumbled in his sleep, and whose leg shot out sometimes, as if he were chasing a rabbit? Was that how his mother and Ceese were loving each other right now, even if they were just sitting at the kitchen table still, having coffee?

Ms. Nordstrom was engaged; she wore a ring on her left hand. She was going to marry an airline pilot and travel to the rain forest and the desert and the mountains. The last time Edgar saw her, when he had told her he was moving to the Yukon, she had been excited. "Your eyes are going to stretch wide, wide!" she'd said.

He didn't say, "But you will not be there."

He didn't say, "But now I won't be able to look at you."

He remembered now more clearly. They had been in a hurry to get to the airport, but he had insisted he wanted to say good-bye to Ms. Nordstrom. His mother had waited in the noisy school lobby, and he and Ms. Nordstrom had stood in the hallway outside the classroom. He could make it all happen again in his head but without the noise. Ms. Nordstrom wasn't wearing her red turtleneck; her shoulders were hidden beneath a ski sweater. Just for a moment when he had waved to her from outside her open door, her eyes had grown large. He had been away for a few days. That wasn't so unusual, yet she'd seemed to recognize that something was happening.

When she came out, he explained to her briefly, and then it became normal and she was able to say, "Your eyes are going to stretch wide, wide!"

Was that her way of loving him?

The classroom had been empty. Everybody must have been at gym class with Mr. Weiskopf, whose whistle shrieked and who was often angry. Ms. Nordstrom would've made an excellent phys ed teacher, but she also needed time to prepare for other classes. That must have been what she was doing at her desk when he stood outside the door and waved.

Benjamin startled awake, and Edgar said, "You would have liked Ms. Nordstrom."

"Who?" Benjamin woofed.

"My old teacher. She let me sit at the back and read whatever I wanted, and then during recess we would talk about it."

Benjamin sniffed Edgar's hand, farted, got up for a moment and turned around and around tumultuously, then settled back down. "Never went to school," he said.

"I guess I'm going to have to go," Edgar said, even though it was fine right there. A stretch of light was just beginning to curl through the window and rest on Benjamin's silky black tail.

(Was this his own sort of dream, then? Edgar wondered. As soon as he thought again of what his mother and Ceese were probably doing, of the hardness and shock that would certainly follow, then Ms. Nordstrom disappeared, his throat retightened, a coldness took over his skin.)

Edgar moved reluctantly toward the new not-theirs house. A glint of hope—Ceese's truck, which had been parked outside, was gone. The sun had shifted to higher in the sky, but it felt dull on Edgar's face. He had an odd moment pausing in front of the door, as if he might need to knock. The house still felt strange to him. Was there any air at all? But he walked in and began to take off his jacket.

"Where have you been?" His mother sounded worried. Her shirt was untucked; she had a small smear of lipstick near the corner of her mouth, and so he knew.

Already it had happened!

Edgar's insides twisted even further. He had a hard time meeting her eyes; his fingers became clumsy over the laces of his boots.

His mother loomed over him, her arms crossed. She had brushed her hair. Edgar must have happened in before she could get herself completely together again.

But Ceese's truck was gone. Edgar imagined his mother lying by herself for a time, dreaming, lost.

He bit his lip. But still his fingers stayed clumsy.

"Where were you?" she asked again.

"I took Benjamin for a walk." The words were clear in his mind; he used his lips the way he always did to make such words. Nothing at all felt different. Yet even he heard himself say instead, "Woof! Woof!"

"Don't you try to be funny with me!" his mother said. She could become angry in a blink. Maybe things had not gone so well with Ceese after all. Sometimes, after she had been with a man, she seemed torn, like a sheet of metal, jagged and coming apart.

"I wasn't being funny," he said.

But what came out instead, again, was, "Woof! Woof-woof!" He rubbed his mouth with his hand as if that could get his muscles back to working properly.

"Edgar," she said dangerously.

He didn't try to make another sound. He was twisting inside, heating from his boots on up, but he didn't want to move. If he stayed very still, sometimes she just went away and he could be himself for a while.

"I don't like you just disappearing like that," she said finally. "Did you walk the dog? Is that what you were doing? For three hours?"

He nodded his head, kept his eyes large. His tongue was stiff and nervous. He swallowed, and everything tasted strange.

"You can make yourself a sandwich if you'd like," she said, turning back to the kitchen. "You must be hungry."

When she was all the way in the kitchen, he tried, quite successfully, to make a barking noise.

"Why are you doing that?" she asked, but in a walking-away tone, as if she didn't expect an explanation.

"I don't know," he said, but now the sound came out in a doggy sort of whine.

He took off his boots and put them and his winter coat in the closet. He was hungry, or at least he used to be. But he shut himself in the bathroom and looked at his mouth and throat in the mirror. *What is going on?*

"Just talk normal," he said urgently.

"Woof-woof, woof-woof-woof!"

He whispered, barely moving his lips: "You're acting like it's a dream."

"Rrrrrrrrrrrrrrrrrrrrr."

He shut his eyes, shook his head, bit the inside of his cheek.

When he opened his eyes, he still looked like himself in the mirror.

If he had turned into a dog, then he would smell things

much more powerfully. *(How could he even be having these thoughts? Yet he was!)* He sniffed the bar of soap his mother had put out. It was wet. He thought he could smell Ceese, his hands.

He couldn't smell any bears from the other side of the hill. But maybe they were sleeping in their caves.

He didn't look like he was becoming a dog.

He let his tongue hang out and he panted for a moment. It did feel oddly nice to do that.

He sniffed the towel hanging on the door—yes, Ceese, definitely. Through his nose he could almost see the memory of him leaning over the sink washing his hands, then splashing water onto his face.

"Talk, talk, talk, talk, talk!" he said.

"Woof-woof, woof-woof-woof!" he heard himself say.

He left the tap dripping, dripping, so that the pipes wouldn't freeze. If this was a dream, would he even remember to do that?

DOCTOR

WAS HE BECOMING A DOG? WAS ANY OF THIS really happening? All the food they had bought—the peanut butter in the cupboard and milk in the fridge, the bread and butter on the table—still smelled tasty to him. His mother found a dish towel for him to use as a napkin, and she said, "We're going to have to get you enrolled in the local school."

He could understand her perfectly. And didn't dogs see in different colors? Everything looked exactly the same as before. Edgar chewed his sandwich and drank his milk nervously.

"You're going to have to be normal when you go to the school," his mother said.

He could smell where Ceese had been sitting, where the two of them had stood close together by the coffeemaker.

It was like he could see a shadow of how things had been hours before. When his mother leaned against the table now, he could smell where Ceese had put his hand on her shoulder.

"You act strange sometimes, but I'm used to it, and you know I'm only saying this for you, don't you?" She looked at him as if her thoughts might somehow dig their way into his eyes. And he wondered, *Saying what?*

I am your mother, her eyes said.

"You can't go around . . . barking, or not saying anything to anyone, or talking about strange things the way you do sometimes and no one understands you," she said.

Edgar gulped.

"You are a strange boy, and that's why people treat you the way they do sometimes. I know you're really smart, but you don't act like it a lot of the time. You act like you don't understand how people work and what makes them want to like you."

Edgar took another bite but didn't move his eyes.

"You have to pay attention to people around you. Act as if you are interested in them, even if you aren't. In the beginning, that's how you get to know who's who. Listen, and smile, and say things sometimes that sound just like everyone else. We all like people who fit in."

He drank the rest of his milk even though he still had

one more piece of bread with peanut butter on it.

"Like right now. You could say something to me right now to indicate you know exactly what I'm telling you."

She stared at him, she stared; he wasn't going to get away with staying silent.

"Woof-woof," he said quietly.

She slammed her hand down on the table, and everything jumped.

"That's exactly what I mean! That wasn't funny! Edgar!"

He swallowed and looked away and tried to gurgle something in his throat that sounded human.

"Talk! God damn you! Talk!"

He looked around desperately. What could—there was a pencil on the counter by the telephone, and little sheets of paper. He got up quickly and wrote, *My throat feels bad.*

When she read the note, he knew she did not believe him. He also could smell Ceese on her neck. He kept himself from sniffing closer, even though the whole story of it was slathered on her.

"Open up." She grabbed him by the back of his hair, and he opened his mouth so she could look. "Say 'ahh.'"

He whimpered, he grumbled, woofed.

"You're faking it!" she said, letting him go. "How

many times do you do this to me? Pretending to be sick just when we need to fit in and not make trouble?"

His face was baking. He needed to pee suddenly. He couldn't tell her, and he couldn't write it in a note, not the way she was feeling. She might slap him. So he ran to the bathroom again and shut the door quickly, locked it, then stood over the toilet with relief.

If he were a dog, he would pee outside. He would raise his leg.

If he were a dog, he would not have been able to write the note.

He flushed the toilet and washed his hands—all very human actions—and then sat down on the toilet seat and smelled again where Ceese had washed his own hands. It was like a ghost of him was there still, like the story kept playing out even after it was over.

His mother knocked on the door. "Edgar?" she said.

A dog would not be able to sit on the toilet like this.

"Edgar, I'm sorry," she said. "It's just, so much has happened. I'm not surprised you're upset. Maybe you *are* sick. Maybe you picked up something on the plane. I can take you to the clinic if you like. It's just down the hill. I remember Ceese telling us. I need to get out anyway."

She waited. There was nothing she could do with the door locked. He could smell her in the bathroom, too, and something else, maybe the faint ghosts of the Summer-hills. It was like all these things and people were piled on top of one another in this one little room where so much happened and you weren't supposed to know.

Dr. Gumstul had large cheeks and a red streak in her hair, as if she had ducked her head yet still run into a paint-brush. The health center was the new building just down the hill from the house, and there had been hardly any wait. Edgar could still feel the cold air from his jacket as he sat in the small examining room.

Edgar's mother said, "His throat is sore, he says. He's been barking like a dog."

Dr. Gumstul smiled a little bit. "What kind of dog? A husky? Chihuahua?"

Edgar couldn't say. What kind of dog was Benjamin? A Newfoundland. The huge, black, old, smelly, drooly kind.

The doctor motioned to the examining table that was covered in white paper. "Could you sit here for me, Edgar, and take off your coat and shirt?"

Edgar loosened himself from his layers, mounted the table slowly.

"Please open your mouth." The doctor took a narrow flashlight from her pocket and shone it down his throat. If he really were a dog, he thought, he might try to bite her.

She touched the sides of his neck with warm fingertips.

"I don't see any signs of inflammation," she murmured.

Her stethoscope was cold on his chest.

"Could you cough, please? Edgar?"

"Woof! Woof!"

Edgar's mother crossed the room toward him, then turned away, as if she could barely contain herself. "Edgar!" she hissed.

"It's fine," Dr. Gumstul said. She tapped his back with her fingers while listening to the stethoscope.

Edgar's mother glared at him with her arms crossed. The doctor stared into his ears, then took his temperature.

"Is your throat actually sore, Edgar?" the doctor asked.

She smelled of oranges, of a long walk in the snow, of something musty in her car.

Edgar shook his head slightly.

"Tell her!" his mother blurted. "Tell her, in words, what you're feeling!"

Edgar stared at his boots.

Dr. Gumstul asked Edgar's mother if she would mind if she had a private word just with Edgar. Edgar didn't know if his mother would leave—she seemed to be holding a pot of boiling water. "Fine," she said, after a moment.

But she motioned to the doctor to join her. Dr. Gumstul told Edgar to put his shirt back on. Then they closed the door, yet Edgar could still hear them out in the hallway. Maybe it was his doggy ears, or just the way his mother's voice carried.

"I didn't take much care when I was pregnant," she said. "It's my fault. I was young and stupid. He's supersmart, but he really isn't entirely right in the head."

"In what way?" the doctor asked.

"He's in his own world. God knows what he's thinking most of the time. But I just love him no matter what."

"I'm sure you do. Has he had any sort of diagnosis?"

"He's been tested—oh, he's been tested!" Edgar's mother replied. "Everybody's so impressed. But he thinks and thinks, and a lot of the time nothing actually comes out. I think the diagnosis you're looking for is that he's just plain weird."

If Dr. Gumstul replied, Edgar didn't hear it. In a moment she knocked on the door and returned to Edgar's side. She bent down to look Edgar in the eye. "What *are* you feeling, Edgar?"

Edgar shrugged his shoulders.

"I understand you've just arrived in Dawson. Have you been this far north before?"

Edgar opened his mouth, then closed it. He could

hear actual words in his mind, but inside all he could feel was barking noises.

"Are you anxious about starting school here?"

The doctor's teeth were big, all of them, and very white. But not thoughtful at all.

"Maybe you left a lot of friends back home?" She smiled. Edgar smelled mayonnaise.

"Is there something you want to tell me, Edgar? Did something happen to you back in Toronto?"

The doctor had dark flecks in her light brown eyes.

"Has anybody hurt you, Edgar?"

The room smelled strongly of chemicals but also of traces of people, too many to count, who had all been here, maybe sitting exactly like Edgar was now.

Edgar wasn't sure his lips could form regular words. How to make them?

How could he forget from one moment to the next?

"Edgar, do you understand what I'm saying?"

Edgar nodded. It was something to know about adults: they will insist and insist, but eventually they go away and leave you alone.

"There are people you could talk to, people who can help," Dr. Gumstul said. "I'd be happy to make an appointment for you. I know someone who is excellent with children. Would you like to meet her? Would that be a good idea? She comes up here from Whitehorse once every two months."

They wanted you to agree—most adults did—and then they would leave you alone.

"Edgar?" the doctor said.

On the walk back up the hill, Edgar's mother said, into cigarette smoke that choked his nose, "Could you just please, please, Edgar, just be normal while we're here? I have such a good feeling about this place. It's really important for me right now to have a sense of safety, of belonging, to start again fresh and be with people"—puff, puff—"who are loving and open and don't judge me and put me in some little box I don't fit into. I hate that! I won't put up with it anymore. So I'm not going to. And I need you to just be quiet, normal, ordinary, adorable"—puff, puff—"Edgar while we're here. All right? Can I count on you, Edgar?"

Edgar said, "Is Ceese the new Roger?"

But it came out, "Woof! Woof-woof-woof!"

"Edgar!" His mother threw away her cigarette and put her gloved hands to her head like she was in a cartoon.

He couldn't help himself. The words just spilled out: "He has a Victoria already. You've met her, even!"

Or, more exactly: "Woof-woof! Woof-woof-woof-woof-woof-woof!"

She might hit him if he continued—he knew it, and yet part of him wanted to make her explode, just blow up right there in the street in front of everybody.

Everybody?

The street was empty. He was alone with his mother, as always. So he clamped his jaw. He walked the rest of the way up the hill, making himself as small and as quiet as he possibly could.

BROTTINGER

CAROLINE BROUGHT BENJAMIN OVER LATER in the day. She was carrying his leash balled up in her hand while Benjamin walked free, even along the slippery boards of the drawbridge. Edgar spied them coming and opened the door.

"Smells like dinner," Benjamin said. The house was still filled with food smells, from the omelette breakfast to last night's casserole. And Edgar remembered he had been in Dawson for only a day. It already felt like it had been much longer.

Caroline was pulling a wagon behind her with a large bag of dry dog food, several cans of meat for dogs, and an old shaggy blanket that smelled thoroughly of Benjamin.

"The Summerhills promised, so here's Benjamin," Caroline said. "Maybe we could share or something?"

Edgar nodded. She didn't seem to be sad about joint custody. Maybe she was used to making accommodations.

"Do you want to take him for a walk now?" Caroline asked. "I'll show you the dog park."

Edgar's mother was back in her bedroom getting ready for her first evening of work at Lola's. Edgar thought about leaving her a note but decided she would see the wagonload of Benjamin's supplies in the front hall and would know what he was doing.

He pulled on his coat and boots as quickly and quietly as he could.

"I'm trying to do this stupid project with your very favorite person, Jason Crumley," Caroline said when they were walking along Eighth Avenue, heading vaguely in the direction of the big gouge in the mountainside. The slide—Moosehide. "Do you do a lot of group projects in school in Toronto? Because I hate them. The history of the Internet. Like—who cares? Just as long as it works!"

Benjamin was walking better. He seemed to enjoy listening to Caroline. He stopped at one snow-covered pee rock, which Edgar found himself sniffing, too. It was hard to tell how many dogs had marked it—eighteen? Twenty? A whole furry mess of them, males and females, old ones, puppies, harsh, happy, jealous, cold. And one huge one. Edgar could feel he was almost a wolf just from his scent, much stronger than everyone else's.

"Brottinger," Benjamin muttered. "You'll want to stay clear of him!"

Edgar could almost picture the harsh yellow teeth, the enormous haunches, the sharp grin.

"What are you doing?" Caroline said.

Edgar straightened up. It made a difference to bend closer to the news. (It was like reading the news, he thought—sniffing a good pee rock with Benjamin.)

He was sure he would be able to speak normally around her. "You can tell a lot just from sniffing," he said, perfectly.

Benjamin started forward again.

"Why are you barking at me?" Caroline asked.

Edgar's heart plummeted. Really? He couldn't even talk to Caroline anymore? But the words had sounded fine to him!

What, what, what is happening?

"Bark all you want around Benjamin. I don't care," Caroline said. "But I sure don't speak dog!"

Edgar felt queasy. This strangeness would take thinking, it would take time to figure out.

How was he ever going to tell her about her father and his mother?

The big dog, the scary one, Brottinger, was all along

Eighth Avenue, and then down the hill, everywhere—at least his scent was. It was like burned coffee, or something scalded in the pan.

"The thing I really hate about Jason Crumley," Caroline said, "is that he thinks he's so smart. He's been the smartest kid in the class since grade one, so he thinks he knows everything. And he's got a slap shot. Who cares? When he shoots the puck, the goalie gets out of the way. Hockey's over anyway, why is he still talking about it?"

Someone had left a liquor bottle in the snow. Benjamin licked and nuzzled it until Caroline put it into her pocket. "Last thing we need is a drunk dog!" she said.

If he had brought paper and a pen, Edgar could have written her a note—about Ceese and Edgar's mother, what was going to happen—but she would ask questions, wonder how he knew and what he thought they should do about it. And why he was writing everything anyway.

She said, "Jason Crumley tried to get me drinking from something up behind the *George Black*, but I told him forget it, I wouldn't trust him with anything in a bottle. He thinks he's king crap. It's a big race against himself, is what my mother says."

Maybe there was nothing they could do anyway. Maybe Edgar needed to just stay quiet.

He smelled the ghosts of other animals along whatever road they were on now, heading down toward the town, and yet away from it as well, circling toward the ancient rock slide. What could he smell? Something wild that could've been fox, and maybe—something larger. What was—

"Bear," Benjamin sniffed. "Came along here last night."

It smelled massive, stinky—

"Nothing reeks like bear," Benjamin said.

Caroline stopped now to look at the large black frozen lumpy pile. "Bear scat," she said. "I guess they're starting to wake up."

Benjamin kept sniffing it and sniffing.

"Probably from now on you should bring some bear spray with you if you walk Benjamin alone on the trails," Caroline said. "But he'll protect you." She nuzzled Benjamin, who didn't raise his head. "Won't you, boy?"

The dog park was a slow walk away, close to the river and on the edge of town: a fenced-off area near mounds and mounds of snow. Caroline said all those mounds were the dumping ground for the city snowplows. Edgar was looking up, up, away from the mounds. They were nearly at the base of the slide, a huge rubble of snow-covered boulders stretching so far above them. Why hadn't he brought his camera?

Because he was smelling everything. That was new.

When they were inside the fence, Caroline said, "I don't believe it," and her face flushed even beyond the red smartness brought on by the cold. Edgar sniffed him first, felt hair stiffening on the back of his neck—where he had no hair, none that he knew of.

"Brottinger," Benjamin mumbled. He coughed and drooled on the side of a bench.

Brottinger was gray and white, pretty big but still smaller than Benjamin, it looked like. He was digging at the base of a large rock, with a boy standing nearby.

"Jason Crumley," Caroline announced, "and that dog of his. The only mean Alaskan malamute I've ever met. Benjamin—come on!" She pulled on the dog's leash, but now Brottinger had spied them. He barked fiercely and bounded over. Even though he was bigger, Benjamin lay down before Brottinger and began rolling in the snow.

"Get up! Get up, Benjamin!" Caroline said.

Brottinger had a low, snarly voice. "Who said you could come to the park now?" he snapped. "Don't you know I'm here?"

Benjamin exposed his belly and, smiling, waved his legs in the air.

"Don't be so pathetic!" Caroline muttered.

Jason Crumley looked their way, and Edgar felt a hollow queasiness. Then Brottinger noticed Edgar, who pulled back his cheeks, but it didn't help. "Who are you, who are you?" Brottinger growled. It wouldn't take much for him to tear at Edgar's throat.

Benjamin rolled around some more and said, "We're okay. We're nobody. We love you."

"Get a grip on your stupid dog, Jason!" Caroline called.

The boy headed toward them. He was enjoying the show. "It's an off-leash zone," he called. "Don't go bringing some old fart can't run wild for half a minute."

Brottinger shoved his muzzle straight between Edgar's legs and said, "Smells like meat to me!"

"It's okay. We're all just playing here," Benjamin giggled.

"Meat! Meat! Meat!" Brottinger barked.

Jason slipped the leash onto his dog. "C'mon, Brot." He tugged sharply, but the dog was too strong.

"It's fun! Fun! We're just going!" Benjamin said.

Caroline clenched her fists like she was going to clock someone. Jason was a head taller and looking at her like he would love it if she threw a punch. Like he might try to kiss her for it.

"Go catch the bear, why don't you?" Caroline said when Jason had pulled Brottinger away. Then, when they were a decent distance apart, backs turned, trying not to seem like they were walking away too quickly, Caroline said in a low voice, "That's the only genuinely evil dog in all of Dawson.

They must feed him razor blades and blood soup."

"Just keep walking. Keep walking," Benjamin mumbled.

Edgar looked back. Brottinger was running after something, heading in another direction, but Jason was still looking at them, his whole face lit now, laughing.

"You did the right thing just staying still," Caroline said. "A dog like that, you never know what he's going to do. And you, Benjamin!" She had to lengthen her stride to keep up with the old dog. "You're a disgrace to dogdom, you are!"

THINGS

WHEN THEY GOT HOME, EDGAR'S MOTHER had already left for work. She had put Benjamin's food in the kitchen, although not away in the cupboard somewhere—it was piled on the table. Benjamin's blanket was on the floor by Edgar's bed. So Edgar and Caroline filled up a bowl with dog food and another with water, and the three of them settled in Edgar's room. Caroline said she would have to get back soon for dinner, but she wanted to tell Edgar something. It sounded important. Edgar wondered if she knew already about Ceese and Edgar's mother.

Caroline and Edgar were lying on his bed this time. She liked to lie on her front with her chin resting on her hands. "There's this thing," she said. "My mom told me when I was little, but I kind of forgot, and then she told me again when I got older. So I'm telling you, even though you might forget for a while. You have to be pretty well naked."

Edgar wondered for a moment if she was proposing they take off their clothes, for some reason.

Benjamin farted. He snuffled his head onto his paws on the blanket by the bed and seemed to be sleeping.

"Technically, I suppose just your private parts have to be naked," Caroline said. "But a lot of the time people are naked, or mostly naked. That's what you see on the Internet a lot. Are you following me?"

Edgar nodded, as if he were following.

"You have really big eyes," Caroline said. "And you never say much, which I guess I like, since I know you're listening. I liked the way you stood up to Brottinger. You were scared but you didn't let on. I hate that dog so much!"

Benjamin jerked his leg; the bedpost moved. Maybe he was fighting it out with Brottinger, or the bear, in his dream.

"You were scared, but you didn't let it show too much. That's why I'm going to tell you: if Jason Crumley unzipped his fly, he might get me in trouble, his thing in my thing, understand?"

Edgar did know about the nakedness. "The thing in the thing" sounded like an odd way to say it.

"It's supposed to be, like, this whole sexy thing," Caroline said. "You get all hot and sweaty. I know it's hard to imagine. But I can tell you, all this year Jason Crumley has started to bother me. People breathe a lot. Probably you've seen all this on the Internet anyway, coming from Toronto."

Edgar nodded even though mostly he had just tried the Internet from school computers or from the library and mostly it had been about finding books he would like to read. Probably there were books all about the sweating and the sex and the thing into the thing, but he hadn't read any yet. It all felt a bit jumbled in his mind.

"We sure wouldn't do it behind the *George Black*. It's so cold there, and practically public, too! I have no idea why Jason thought I would go drinking with him. It's hard to imagine, when you look at a boy, that there could be much of a thing in there anyway. It's not like the pictures on the Internet. Not that I've seen many! This isn't what our project is going to be about."

She would say anything, this Caroline, and it was kind of warm-making to lie on the bed thinking about what else she might say. Edgar imagined that if he weren't here, she might be having exactly the same conversation with just Benjamin, who might or might not be asleep.

He thought about Jason and Caroline behind the

George Black, which must be a sort of statue or something out in public. If Edgar could have spoken without barking, he would have asked her what exactly the *George Black* was anyway.

But maybe I'm like Benjamin to her, he thought. *Maybe it doesn't matter if I can speak to her or not.*

"Not that it's going to happen," Caroline said. "Jason Crumley is such a jerk, just like his dog almost."

Benjamin's stink had already filled the room. The next fart was almost visible.

It was hard to imagine anyone without clothes, as cold as the day was outside, behind a statue or not. And even inside your house you would want a sweater and warm pants and thick socks.

But since Caroline was talking to him this way, he felt he could tell her about Ceese and his mother, that she would understand. If only the woof-woof wasn't still in his throat!

"I'd better get home for dinner," Caroline said. "Don't be shy if you have any questions about Benjamin or the other thing." She paused so that Edgar had to look at her and indicate he knew exactly what she was talking about. "But as I said, probably you're going to forget anyway. Still, it's good that I told you. You don't want to be a complete imbecile all your life."

She arched her eyebrows—did he understand the word "imbecile"? He thought probably he did. He couldn't help himself, he imagined Ceese and his mother pretty well naked in the big bed in her new room being sweaty, the way Roger and his mother had been, and other men before that, Felipe and Jerome and the one who always read his horoscope in the morning to find out what kind of day it would be.

Sebastian.

Edgar could remember the names of many men his mother had been naked with.

When Caroline left, the house felt suddenly quiet, and Edgar found the bit of last night's moose casserole his mother had left for him to heat up for dinner.

SCHOOL

EDGAR WOKE UP IN DARKNESS WITH HIS blankets kicked off him. His feet especially felt like chilled meat, which made him think of Brottinger yesterday barking, "Meat! Meat! Meat!" right into his privates. And he remembered Caroline telling him about the thing in the thing. It wasn't his first time hearing such a story. It seemed in every new school he went to, some kid took him aside to make sure he knew about the thing in the thing. He couldn't forget about it even if he wanted to.

And you didn't have to do it at all unless you wanted to. Maybe someday he would. For now, that seemed enough to know.

Benjamin was sleeping on his blanket. He sounded like he was happy not to wake up.

So Edgar put on socks and his big brown sweater over

his pajamas and sort of skated his feet toward the bathroom, where he didn't smell anything unusual. He made
sure the taps were still dripping. And he thought: Maybe a
lot of yesterday was a dream, the whole dog-barking bit just
a story that his brain had made up while he was sleeping.

His mother and Ceese, was that a dream too?

He looked in the mirror and said, "My name is Edgar."
And then he said, "Woof. Edgar Woof."

He thought he knew what sounded like a real word
and what sounded doggish.

Maybe everyone else had been dreaming yesterday—
that's why his speech had gotten so reversed. Probably
people talk like dogs all the time in their dreams and it's
no big deal.

It was dark, and yet it was morning—7:17 according
to the digital clock in the kitchen when he got there. He
pulled out a pot and a measuring cup and set the water to
boiling for oatmeal.

"Edgar Woof!" he said again.

He wondered if the bear had had a cold night. Maybe
with that thick fur, bears didn't get very cold at all and
enjoyed wandering around town in the darkness.

Would Brottinger be scared of the bear, or the other
way around? Maybe Brottinger would lie giggling on his
back in front of the bear like Benjamin had in front of him.

A beer bottle was opened on the kitchen table. Edgar didn't smell it right away, so maybe he wasn't a dog after all? But as soon as he saw it, the bottle stank like sweaty, salty socks. Had his mother brought someone home after work? Probably not.

His mother would not be awake for hours.

No point in making the coffee yet. He found the oatmeal in the cupboard and stirred two cups into the boiling water, then turned down the heat. He stared at the map on the fridge for a moment, the old one with West Dawson (abandoned), and Moosehide, too, down the river.

"I can talk just like myself today," he said out loud.

It sounded perfect. He remembered that on Roger's phone he could record himself. If Roger were here now, with his phone, Edgar could record himself and then listen to find out whether words or dog barks came back at him.

If all I can do is bark, he thought, *maybe I won't have to go to school.*

Was there such a rule? No dogs in school, to be sure.

Maybe he could just sit in the back of the class and bark to himself and read.

Later Ceese was at the door. Edgar flung it open and said, "Thank you for letting me have Benjamin!" but Ceese's face was not right. He looked like a man being barked at by a kid.

"Good morning to you, too!" he said. "Are you ready to go?"

Go where? Edgar thought, but Ceese was standing there as if they had an understanding.

"Didn't your mother tell you? Maybe she got in too late last night. I saw her at Lola's, and she asked me to take you to school this morning. She was worried she might not wake up in time. Caroline has gone ahead. She has some project she had to do."

Edgar was dressed already. It did not take him long to brush his teeth.

"What have you got for school supplies?" Ceese asked. "A notebook, some pens? You can come home at lunch if you're not slow about it. The school is only a few blocks away."

Edgar hadn't taken Benjamin for his walk yet. What time was it? Could Benjamin wait until noon?

It was hard to get a breath, pulling on his winter things, and thinking also about how disappointing it was to still be barking rather than talking. This was not a dream. He could feel his toes in his boots, already cold even though he hadn't stepped outside. And now there would be a lot of other kids to meet, and he wouldn't be able to say anything!

Suddenly his mother was there in a bathrobe that did not belong to her. She must have found it in the closet of her bedroom. It was silky and it clung tight to where she held it shut, and she didn't seem to mind Ceese looking at her as she hugged Edgar.

"I'm sorry I can't take you myself. It was a good night last night, though. The job is good. You just go and be yourself, all right? You just go and be my beautiful Edgar."

Her breath smelled of beer, but it wasn't a bad smell. Her face was not pale and her hands weren't shaking.

She kissed him on both cheeks, then straightened up and whispered, "Thank you!" to Ceese. Edgar could smell the two of them together. He could feel the heat between them.

He wanted to ask his mother to take Benjamin for a little walk, but he knew the words would not form themselves. What to do? If he had a notebook . . .

"What is it, Edgar?" his mother asked.

Edgar pointed to the stairs heading down to his bedroom, where Benjamin was still sleeping.

"What?"

Edgar knelt to take his boots off. There was a slip of paper in the kitchen he could write on. . . .

"Edgar, tell me! Just open your mouth and tell me!"

Edgar stayed on one knee, his fingers on his laces.

She gripped him by the shoulders and pulled him upright. Her dressing gown began to fall open, so she unclenched him to hold herself. Softly, like a little earthquake, she said, "Edgar."

He had never felt an actual earthquake, little or big, but he had felt the subway in Toronto when they had been staying in a tiny basement apartment near a station.

The kitchen sink had been in the bathroom, that apartment was so small.

Edgar opened his mouth. "Woof."

He didn't want to disappoint her. But she was making him. If Ceese had not been there, she might have slapped him even though it was morning and she wasn't drunk.

"What's that?" Ceese said.

"He's barking," his mother said. "Instead of talking, he's barking like a dog." She took Edgar's face in her big right hand. "Don't think you're going to get out of school pulling this stunt. I'm tired of it, do you understand? I'm here to start a new life. The least you can do is go to school and open your mouth and talk. All right?"

When she released him, he fell backward a couple of steps. Ceese had to catch him to keep him from falling over.

Edgar's whole body was hot, hot. His jaw was so clamped shut, he didn't think he would be able to open it for anyone.

"It's all right. It's going to be fine," Ceese said, but even his voice rattled in the moment.

Outside, the air was cold and the smells came back. Edgar didn't know if someone somewhere was flipping a switch, turning him into a dog and then not, but that was what it felt like. And it smelled like a dozen dogs had already been out and had their morning pee along Eighth Avenue and down the hill. Brottinger was not one of them. Maybe he lived in a different part of town and only sometimes came up here. And the bear smell was a little old, so the bear hadn't been out in the night, as far as Edgar could tell.

Ceese walked beside him. He had a proper jacket on now but no gloves or hat. He didn't seem to feel the cold the way Edgar did. He said, "What is it with all this barking, anyway?"

Edgar wanted to say, "I don't know, it just came on. It doesn't always sound like barking to me!" But he didn't know what was going to come out, so his jaw stayed glued.

"Was it that business back in Toronto? Your mom told me a bit about what went down with what's his name. Roger, was it?"

Edgar stayed by the side of the road, where it wasn't

so slippery. It was going to be another bright day. The sky looked clear, and once again there was no wind. It felt easy to breathe despite the cold.

"Anything you want to say to me, anytime you want to talk, I'm a good listener!" Ceese said.

It really wasn't very far to the school. In a couple of blocks, when they were down on the flat, they turned right again, toward the Moosehide Slide in the distance. The road was wide, wide. There was room enough for several snow-and-dirt lanes. They walked on the wooden sidewalk, stepping down onto the snow when they had to cross the street. What was it about the look of the school? Obviously, the building had not been here during the gold rush days. It looked more modern, newer but still boxy. Kids were playing, running, shouting in the fenced-in area, all in colorful snowsuits and jackets. Edgar pulled his cheeks back. He hoped the kids would see Ceese but not him.

They mounted the wooden stairs. Ceese pulled open the door for him. "That's the library to the right. Want to have a look?" They had to take their boots off and go through another set of doors. It seemed fine, this library: shelves and shelves of books; lots of windows, too; an upstairs with even more books. And many places to be quiet and hide.

Ceese introduced him to the librarian on duty, a woman named Lucetta who smelled of toast and jam and something sickly. It was hard to know what it was. Her face was a little gray. "Edgar's brand-new today!" Ceese announced. "He and his mom just came in from Toronto. First time in the Yukon! But he's got an eye for books, I can just tell. Don't you, Edgar?"

Edgar nodded. He was eager to go along the bookshelves, looking at the titles and the covers.

"What grade are you in, Edgar?" Lucetta asked.

Edgar felt his throat constrict, his face flush.

Ceese and Lucetta were both looking at him. So he held out four fingers, not in an obvious way, but they could see what he was doing. He was small for his age, and he liked seeming younger. It was another way to hide. Still, he thought about adding more fingers. . . .

"No need to be so shy here," Lucetta said. She bent down so that her face was close to his and he had to look into her eyes, which were red-rimmed, a bit sad. "Everyone is really friendly here."

They accepted it.

So Edgar nodded. He felt himself trying to smile, like someone posing for a picture but who does not know what he is pretending to feel.

They left the library, put their boots back on, and

then pushed through another set of doors that led into the noisy halls of the school. It all looked familiar. How many schools had he been to in just the last few years? Usually his mother came with him, but not always. Sometimes she expected him to just introduce himself to the principal and she would come later to fill out the paperwork.

This principal was short and wide, with a grinning face and a shirt that did not quite stay tucked in on the side where his belly spilled over his belt: Mr. Trant. He shook Edgar's hand formally, and when Ceese said Edgar was from Toronto, Mr. Trant talked for several minutes about the Maple Leafs and what a sorry hockey team they were. "It's the corporate influence. I know everyone says it, but it's true—they never have to have a good team because all the seats get sold anyway! Still, it's hard not to watch them. They're like a slow-motion train wreck, Saturday night after Saturday night. But a great thing about living in the Yukon is the time shift. You can watch the Leafs lose and still have time to do something else in the evening!"

Edgar had never been to a hockey game. Although, of course, in Toronto he had heard lots of people talking about the Leafs. He nodded, and shook his head, and looked at Ceese when Ceese said something about the goaltender. And then Ceese said, "Edgar is looking to join the grade-four class. His mother is going to come by later with all the paperwork. I'm just hoping maybe we can get him started right away. Is Marie-Claire still teaching that group?" Mr. Trant said that she was, and Ceese said to Edgar that he was in for a treat. "Everybody falls in love with Marie-Claire," he said. "I wish I could go back to grade four again!"

"You'd have to learn to sit still, Ceese, I'm afraid," Mr. Trant said, and Ceese shook his head in mock sadness.

"I'd never make it through!"

So it was arranged. No one complained. He *was* small, smaller than average. Marie-Claire too—Ms. Lajoie, which meant "joy," Edgar remembered from his scattered French classes—was shorter than Ms. Nordstrom and had dark hair that clung to her very pretty face. She smelled of fierce joy, as if she had just walked miles through the bush, loving every breath of cold air. That was the feeling Edgar got as he breathed her in, when he was shaking her warm hand a few steps inside her classroom. The children looked at him, of course they did, but he felt himself falling into her kindly eyes and did not let himself look away quite yet. "It is a pleasure to meet you, Edgar!" she said rather formally, with a trace of a French accent. "Where would you like to sit?"

Ceese took her aside, and they spoke as if they were old friends. Ceese was explaining Edgar's shyness, that he would need to be quiet as he got used to the new circumstances.

She had an easy smile, and though she was not tall like Ms. Nordstrom, her neck was long, a little like a swan's, and she held herself straight, perhaps like a dancer.

Edgar was supposed to find a seat, but how could he? He was looking at Ms. Lajoie. He was feeling already the way he had with Ms. Nordstrom, like walking out of a dark place and into sunshine. A word popped into his head: "easement." What did that mean? Maybe this feeling of melting and feeling at ease with the world.

He would be able to speak normal words with Ms. Lajoie, with Marie-Claire. (How her name rang like a bell!) He would.

She turned to him now. Ceese was gone. "Why don't you take your seat, Edgar? How about this one?" She pointed to the very first seat at the front, close to the door.

"Thank you. I am so pleased to be here," he said.

He heard the words perfectly pronounced, and yet part of him also heard what the rest of the class reacted to: "Woof! Woof-woof! Woof!"

Cackles of laughter, a most alarmed expression on Ms. Lajoie's face.

"What was that, Edgar?"

His lips screwed tight. "Hmmm-hghgh," he said, and dropped his eyes, and boiled inside.

How could this be happening to me? How could—

Edgar sat hard in his new seat and held his face in his hands. Ms. Lajoie was speaking, the class continued. For a time it was all noise in his head. Gradually he started to peer between his fingers. A poster on the wall close to him showed a colorful, expanding column of galaxy gas, or something else from outer space. Edgar had seen similar photos in a book at the Toronto Reference Library, where he used to go sometimes when his mother was shopping and wanted an hour to herself.

His blood still surged beneath the skin of his face. He wished, with all his powers, that he would wake up soon and it would be morning again and he would be in his old bed in Toronto.

Maybe . . . maybe he would still have his camera, though. Maybe that part of the dream he could keep, and Benjamin, too, and Caroline. Was it possible that in a dream you could feel like you have lived several days and traveled a great long distance and become a dog-boy?

"Edgar," Ms. Lajoie said. "We're going to be hearing from a number of students today in what we call interest talks, prepared presentations on some subject of their own personal interest. I don't want to put you on the spot, but

I'm hoping that at some point you will feel comfortable telling us just a bit about the city where you've come from. In some ways Toronto and Dawson couldn't be more different, wouldn't you say?"

He could not pull back his cheeks. He was stuck at his new desk being stared at.

Everything real, real.

A girl named Vanessa with red-streaked hair—who looked somehow, in the shape of her face and the paleness of her skin, like she might be the daughter of the librarian—stood up first and talked about her favorite book, *Mr. Marbles's Mushrooms*, which she clutched to her chest while she talked. She also swayed, as if she were singing a song, and didn't quite keep her eyes open.

"Mr. Marbles marries Margery Mushroom, and their children aren't Marbles. Well, some of them are, but some of them are Mushrooms, because Mr. Marbles agreed to share everything when they got married, even names. So she changed her name to 'Marbles' and he changed his name to 'Mushroom,' and their children, some came out Marbles and some Mushrooms, and even some Mushroom-Marbles, while others were clearly Marble-Mushrooms. And when they went to school, it was hard to keep clear who was what because they all borrowed each other's clothes. Then one day Maryellen

Mullins-Maxwell-Moffat, their cousin, came to visit their town called Milford. . . ."

She was tapping her foot too while she was telling the story. She wore a thin red sweater and a bright purple scarf.

"You only have five minutes, dear," Ms. Lajoie said when Vanessa had been talking for some time. Edgar thought: *Maybe if she talks the entire period, I won't have to say anything about Toronto.*

But she didn't talk the whole period. A boy named Salvadore gave a demonstration of card tricks he had learned from his uncle, who was a professional dealer in Las Vegas, where he was not allowed to do card tricks but had to be strictly honest all the time. Still, he did know how to draw an ace every time from the bottom of the deck, or the top, or anywhere, really, and it could be the ace of spades every time too if he wanted. Salvadore was taller than many of the other children and not fast with the cards the way his uncle probably was. Edgar was reminded of playing poker with Roger for nickels, which Roger had kept in a double plastic bag. No matter how much or how little they'd played, Roger had always won all the nickels. But he had taken the time to teach Edgar some of the rules, about full houses and flushes and when diamonds are wild.

"Edgar?" Ms. Lajoie finally said when Edgar was convinced she had forgotten about him, maybe even couldn't see him anymore. "Why don't you tell us a few things about life in Toronto? Did you ride the subway? Or the streetcar?"

She waited at the front of the class, her face full of expectation. It was if she were holding out a plate of treats he knew he would drop as soon as it reached his hand.

A wretched moment of silence. "There is a very tall building in Toronto, isn't there?" she said finally. "What's it called?"

One of the boys shot up his hand. Ms. Lajoie ignored him, but still the boy said, "The CN Tower!"

"Thank you, Rémy. I didn't ask you, did I?"

Edgar didn't look to see if Rémy was embarrassed. The whole room smelled like it was full of laughter not yet happening—swallowed up, strangled.

Edgar stared at one tile on the floor. It was gray-purple, if that was a color. No. Lighter than that. But a lot of feet had darkened it over time. Could he smell all those feet? They filled his mind somehow as he waited for his new teacher to insist that he stand up in front of everyone and say something—anything—about his old home.

Ms. Lajoie was looking at him, looking. He didn't have a notebook, but the girl sitting on his left seemed to have several, and even some extra pens and pencils. He reached across and pulled a notebook and pen toward him, thanking her with his eyes. Then on the back blank page he wrote: *My throat got raw on the airplane. Toronto has a lot of trees and cars. Sometimes I rode in one too. A car. Not a tree.*

He lifted his eyes finally, stood, and handed the notebook to Ms. Lajoie. She thanked him as he was sitting down again. Then she read aloud his note.

When she finished, she looked around and with her eyes kept the class from erupting with laughter. "Welcome to Dawson, Edgar," she said. "I think you'll find we have more trees here than cars. And thanks for telling me about your throat. We won't ask you to do too much talking today."

CAVE

AT RECESS EDGAR WAITED, WAITED FOR MS. Lajoie to invite him to stay inside and read, because of his throat, but she didn't, so he went outside with everyone else. The sun was higher now, the sky too blue to seem real, somehow—impossible in Toronto. But not impossible for here. The hills shone white, with dark pinpricks of trees, and the ravens circled, circled, as if for the joy of being able to, high above everything, close to the sun.

It was possible to stand at the fence and just look.

Caroline found him alone and said, "How's Benjamin?" Edgar wanted to tell her that he had failed in his first duty, that Benjamin had not gotten a walk this morning and now he was suffering or he had peed on the floor of the beautiful borrowed house. But Edgar didn't—he couldn't—open his mouth. It was a useful story that his throat was raw. His throat was even beginning to feel that way, now that he had written such a lie to his brand-new teacher, who had a kind heart. Edgar felt it was so.

"Forget anything I told you about Jason Crumley and all that kissing nonsense," Caroline said to him. "He's just a jerk, which is what my mother said grade-eight boys were going to be like. They are the way they are. You wait it out. Things get better eventually." She was looking at him too closely. "Are you, like—not talking to anybody anymore? 'Cause your mother dragged you all the way up here?"

If only he had brought a notebook and pen with him! He would have explained everything to Caroline. She would have understood it all, even if he had said, "I think I'm turning into a dog." But he wasn't turning into a dog, not really. Part of him was doggy, and part of him was just the same. Mainly he just couldn't speak anything but dog.

Caroline would understand that, wouldn't she?

Somebody called for Caroline, and she drifted off to talk to some big kids lounging around a frozen basketball hoop, near where the sun was fairly strong. Edgar watched a light brown, shaggy dog sniff along a row of houses across the street, not looking up. She was quite far away, but somehow Edgar knew she was heavy with puppies. He felt he had smelled her along the street up near the house on Eighth. When he closed his eyes, he could smell her even better. He had a sense of himself shrinking, getting closer to the ground, becoming furrier . . . and then just trotting away, no one giving a care if he came or went.

It would be nice to be a dog. Just at this very moment.

The bell rang, and the yelling, running, playing kids headed back to the doors in their colorful winter jackets and tall warm boots. Edgar waited by the fence and watched them, wondering now if indeed he had been transformed into a dog and so was excused. As soon as the doors close, he thought, and the yard was empty except for him, he would trot off and find that light brown dog and ask her what she was sniffing about, between those houses.

The kids filed in. Edgar felt himself becoming warm, the way a dog would beneath a thick coat of fur. The teachers on duty herded the children. All was in order; no one was noticing him.

It would be like one of Salvadore's uncle's card tricks, Edgar thought. To just slip into fur and root around as a dog for a time.

The tall teacher turned, spied him. If he were a dog, if he—

"Hey! You're late already! Get a move on!" the teacher yelled.

No fur, no easy escape. Edgar ran, like a boy, toward
the closing doors.

The doors shut behind him, and Edgar hurried along
the hallway. Kids all around him were wrestling off their
winter coats and boots and scampering into their proper
classrooms. His room was . . . somewhere. He thought it
was just along this way and then around the corner, but
that was the kindergarten classroom he'd almost turned
into. Edgar retraced his steps as the halls got quieter . . .
and then he was alone again, lost. There was the office. It
would've been a simple thing to pop in and say, "I'm sorry,
I'm just new. I've forgotten where Ms. Lajoie's room is,"
and someone would have given him directions or walked
him back. It would have been simple for anyone, perhaps,
but not for him, not in his current state.

The tall teacher who had herded him back into the
school was gone now, disappeared to his own duties,
maybe. And now Edgar was back at the front doors.
He could simply walk out again, he realized. No alarm
would go off. But he turned instead where he remembered the library was. He hung his coat on a hook by
the door, pulled off his boots, walked in socked feet
through the doors. Other kids were there, sitting silently
at tables, absorbed in books or in working. The comput-

ers along the wall were occupied. No one looked at him.

He was good at disappearing. He pulled back his cheeks. He melted into nothing practically as he eased his way between the shelves of books. Maybe Ms. Lajoie would just forget that he was her new student and carry on with the lessons for the day.

He spied Lucetta, the librarian with the gray face and red-rimmed eyes, absorbed in something on her computer at the main desk. She did not have to see him. She did not have to look up . . . as he climbed the stairs to the second level, where more books were. Like: *Race Across the Top of the World*. Sled dogs on the cover. He carried it to a small table in a back corner, and then he spied another book, *The Collected Short Stories of Jack London*. So he took that one, crawled under the table, and pulled the chair into place so that he would be safe.

Here. Here it was: "To Build a Fire."

> *Day had dawned cold and gray when the man turned aside from the main Yukon trail. He climbed the high earth-bank where a little-traveled trail led east through the pine forest. It was a high bank, and he paused to breathe at the top. He excused the act to himself by looking at his watch. It was nine*

o'clock in the morning. There was no sun or
promise of sun, although there was not a
cloud in the sky. It was a clear day. However,
there seemed to be an indescribable darkness
over the face of things. That was because the
sun was absent from the sky. This fact did
not worry the man. He was not alarmed by
the lack of sun. It had been days since he had
seen the sun.

As soon as Edgar started to read, he felt himself back
on the Yukon River with his mother, just yesterday, before
Ceese had arrived in his truck, when it had been only the
two of them with their new groceries, and the town had
disappeared. They might as well have been alone with the
ice and the hills and the high, high sky—

"Edgar!" Ms. Lajoie said suddenly. She was kneeling
on the carpet, her face inches from his own. He had not
heard her approach at all. At his name he bonked his head
on the underside of the table. "What are you doing here?"

"I forgot how to get to the classroom!" Edgar
blurted, forgetting himself. Then he waited, in fear, for
her reaction.

"Why are you barking at me?" she said finally.

He stared at the page where the man was heading

toward his doom, but that would be much later. For now he was just a strong fellow out for a walk in the very, very cold.

Ms. Lajoie looked at him; she looked at him. He thought the truth at her until finally she blurted, "My God, you really can't talk! Am I right?"

Edgar nodded, nodded, a little bit.

She disappeared, then came back again with paper and a pen and crawled in under the table beside him. "Tell me," she said. "Write it out."

Edgar closed *The Collected Short Stories of Jack London* and used it to support the paper.

I don't know why, but I just started barking. Benjamin is my new dog. Though he is old. He is new to me. I can talk to him and I can smell things like a dog can too.

She smelled like the last breath of a long walk in cold air, like sharp worry, like she wanted another cup of coffee.

"Has this happened before?"

No.

He thought for a moment.

But I did know it was going to happen. Or, I knew I was going to be able to speak with Benjamin. As soon as I heard about him, I knew. When we were heading up here. He is sick and old, but he is friendly and good to talk to.

It was easy now to sit and write to Ms. Lajoie. His pen blurred along.

I'm sorry for my handwriting. I have never been a good student. I didn't think when I started talking with Benjamin that I wouldn't be able to speak like a boy anymore. It might be just a dream.

Her lips curled into a smile as she read. She was very beautiful. He was lucky that way to have such beautiful teachers. First Ms. Nordstrom, now Ms. Lajoie.

"Do you feel like you are in a dream right now, Edgar?"

It felt like he was alone in a cave with someone who meant him kindness, but she also had to get back to her class. Who was looking after them? That bit of worry leaked from her even while she was pretending she had all the time in the world to spend in quiet like this with a new boy who barked.

I don't know, he wrote. About the dream.

She sat still. He wasn't sure what else to write.

"We're going to need to go back to the classroom," she said finally. "And I'm going to need to talk with your mother. But for now your secret is safe with me, all right?"

Ms. Nordstrom's eyes were very blue, but Ms. Lajoie's were a combination of many colors, of green and brown and blue and maybe gold, too, which would only make sense, since this was a land for gold.

SKURD

EDGAR RAN HOME AT LUNCHTIME. MAYBE his mother would have lunch ready, maybe it would be macaroni, but mostly he had to get home quickly for Benjamin. Also, he was kind of in love already with Ms. Lajoie, who knew his secret. He hadn't just written it; he had thought the truth at her. Also, she had not told anyone else. She had continued for the rest of the morning to teach and to hand out exercises. She had even allowed Edgar to sign out *The Collected Short Stories of Jack London* and to read more of "To Build a Fire" quietly when he was done filling in the missing words and all the number chains on the sheet.

Maybe lunch would be macaroni?

He burst through the door. He felt like he didn't need to be careful, that the world was softer. There was

Victoria, that was true, a storm to come, but it had not hit yet, and maybe Edgar had been fooling himself in imagining the worst.

"Are you talking yet?" his mother called from the kitchen.

He kicked off his boots and showed her the notebook Ms. Lajoie had given him. *I said my throat is raw*, he wrote. *I need to take Benjamin out.*

"I took him already," she said. "He just did his thing in the back. I don't think he likes to walk very far."

It was not macaroni but cut meat and some more powdered cheese and bread with butter, and slices of apple around the edge of the plate. Edgar gobbled it.

"How did it all go?" his mother asked. She seemed happy. She seemed almost as beautiful to him as Ms. Lajoie. He wished he could just think the truth at her and have her know. "Write it out for me if you have to," she said.

She smelled of sleep still, of having traveled a very long way with all that luggage and worry, and now that they were here, the trap that had snapped shut was for some other mouse, not them.

I have a new teacher, and she wants to talk with you, he wrote. *She understands.*

"What does she understand?" his mother asked. Not in a happy tone. Sometimes she could be jealous;

someone else's happiness could crack her own.

The barking is not my fault. I'm just a boy who barks.

He gobbled up the slices of meat, the apple. His mother put her face in her hands. She could not seem to stop looking at him, even through her fingers.

"Where did you come from?" she asked.

But she did not expect an answer. Or that he would write, *From Toronto. With you.*

So he kept eating.

There was only an hour for lunch, and now that had become just twenty-one minutes and he still had to brush his teeth. But he ran down the stairs and woke up Benjamin. "I have a new teacher!" he said. "I can think at her and she knows about me. She let me keep the Jack London book. She doesn't mind if I bark."

"Barking is good," Benjamin said.

"I'm sorry I left before your walk this morning," Edgar said. "I'll come home again right after school."

"Don't bring me to the dog park," Benjamin said. "It stinks of Brottinger."

"Then you show me where," Edgar said.

— — —

The dog did not know anything about temperatures. Possibly in its brain there was no understanding of a condition of very cold, such as was in the man's brain. But the

animal sensed the danger. Its fear made it
question eagerly every movement of the man
as if expecting him to go into camp or to seek
shelter somewhere and build a fire. The dog
had learned about fire, and it wanted fire.
Otherwise, it would dig itself into the snow
and find shelter from the cold air.

— — —

"Hey, you. Where's your camera?"

Edgar looked up. He was sitting with his back to the wall of the school building, in a blob of sunshine, reading during afternoon recess. At first he could not tell who had called after him, but then it became obvious—Jason Crumley was standing opposite him, a water bottle in his hand. The sun was high in the sky behind his face. It was hard to see him clearly.

Edgar would not, could not speak.

Suddenly the book was in Crumley's hands. "What's this crap?" He read aloud, "*The frozen moistness of its breathing had settled on its fur in a fine powder of frost.*"

The sun was so bright behind his face. He just looked like a shadow.

"This a library book?" Crumley held the pages split open in his hands, like he was going to rip it by its spine.

Edgar heard himself growling.

"That supposed to be scary?" Jason Crumley's bulky

jacket was open. He was probably used to hitting people into the boards in hockey games.

That feeling again, that the hair on the back of Edgar's neck was standing up. He squatted now, ready to spring, growled harder. Showed his teeth. Maybe that was why Crumley flipped the book back to him and stepped a few paces off.

Edgar fumbled the catch. The book dropped to the frozen ground. He bent over to pick it up. He knew Crumley could just charge at him—push him over. Edgar felt a strange, quivering ruggedness inside. If that boy got near, he'd just bite his leg.

But when Edgar looked up again, Crumley was gone, disappeared to some other part of the playground.

"I would have bitten him anyway, even if he didn't take the book," Benjamin said later. They were on a wooden boardwalk outside a big closed building called Diamond Tooth Gertie's. Edgar remembered seeing the ad for it at the airport; only, that picture was of women in old frilly dresses kicking up their legs in golden-looking light. This building was drab, deserted. A sign on the door said, GRAND OPENING IN MAY!

A lot of things were still closed for the season, it looked like.

"Wouldn't he just punch me back?" Edgar asked.

It was, still, a pleasant spot to stop and rest. Benjamin closed his eyes in the sun and didn't look cold at all in his thick coat.

"Some of the toughest bites are from small dogs," Benjamin said. "That's why he backed off. It's better when you don't have to fight."

Fart, fart from Benjamin's backside, but a gentle wind took the rot away.

"Did you get in some hard fights yourself?" Edgar asked. He was remembering the way Benjamin had rolled over in front of Brottinger at the dog park. He didn't want to bring it up in case Benjamin was embarrassed.

"Worst was against a yellow dog came shooting out of a trailer. Some dogs hate you just for being big. Brottinger is like that too, hates anyone stands taller than him. Bite your neck just to do it. I swatted the yellow skurd back and back again, but he wouldn't stop coming. Kept trying to chew my tail. I couldn't round fast enough to unclench him."

"What's a skurd?" Edgar asked. What was it about this spot where Benjamin had brought him? It was as if the air, the ground, the place itself were trying to make you feel better just for being there.

"A skurd, a skurd," Benjamin said. "Someone you want to cuff around. Tries to steal your food when he should never eat before you."

Edgar closed his eyes and thought for a moment of the ladies in the old costumes kicking up their legs. That would not be Ms. Lajoie, although she was beautiful.

It felt like all the warmth of those ladies, and the golden light in the picture, was somehow on this very spot where he and Benjamin were resting.

"A skurd too," Benjamin continued, "smells sick so tries to bite you into forgetting. Runs out of the trailer first sniff of a new place. Jumps trying to pee high on a pole. A skurd."

Some ravens flew by; someone parked a truck and walked off toward other buildings. The post office? A bar?

There's a lot of skurdishness, Edgar thought, *in people too.* Pretending, trying to impress. Roger could be like that with his gifts. Even the camera, the way he had handed it over. *I am not losing you and your mother.* Acting somehow, pleading. Like the women in the poster at the airport too? Legs and ruffles and all those smiles. To get you to come in through the drab doors, when just outside, this very spot was pleasant and fresh, perfect for sitting.

"I suppose maybe I used to be a dog," Edgar said. Benjamin nodded, nodded. No one would bother them here. Not with so much still closed.

"It is noble to be one of us," Benjamin said, then settled his head on his paws for a rest.

COMPETITION

"IT'S A GARAGE BAND COMPETITION," EDGAR'S mother said. "I'm not on shift till later in the evening. We'll just go for a little bit. It'll be fun."

Her hair was glistening. She was checking herself in the bathroom mirror, putting on her makeup.

Edgar wrote on his pad, *Are you singing?*

She glanced down from doing something with her eyelids. "I wish you would just go back to talking," she said.

But she got angry when he barked, and probably his voice was still not working. He held up the page a little higher.

"No, of course not. We only just got here. I'm not in anybody's band."

A little later they walked down the hill. It was a cold

evening, the air calm. The hills seemed content, if that was a way to think about it. The hills held themselves against the frozen water, and the town lay still, and a few lights burned as the sky slowly darkened. It was not a big town; that much was clear, the more they walked places. They might change their routes on the grid of streets, but almost everywhere, still, was down the hill from the new house.

"I guess there are a few good musicians in town," his mother said. "Some people have said so. It's one of the great things about working in a bar. People open up, you know? We won't stay long," she said again. "And you'll see, I'm not going to drink much. All that's over for me. This is a brand-new life for both of us. You are enjoying some of it so far, Edgar, aren't you?"

She looked down at him as they walked along. When he didn't speak, she said, "Oh, for God's sake!" and picked up the pace.

His father was a musician, that much he knew. His mother had told Edgar that his father had been in Toronto just for one stretch of shows, and she had not seen or contacted him again. He wasn't famous himself, but he played with famous people. Bass guitar. "At least he's not a drummer!" she had said more than once.

And she was a singer, or she sang sometimes. Not

lately. Roger hadn't liked her performing. He'd get jealous, all those men listening and looking. Edgar liked singing too, but now all he could do was bark! Or maybe howl, too. He hadn't really tried.

Next time with Benjamin, he thought. They could howl some together.

People were gathered on the flat at the big old yellow building. Edgar's mother knew exactly where she was going because it was close to Lola's, the bar where she worked. It was also close to a shop that caught Edgar's eye: Peabody's Photo Parlour. The town had a photo store! But it looked closed up. Still, he stared at the old-fashioned sign. Then his mother was climbing stairs without him, so he hurried to catch up. Inside, another set of stairs led to a large old ballroom—that's what his mother called it—full of chairs now, with the playing area for the bands up front: some microphones and speakers, bright lights, drums and stools.

In a moment his mother held a beer in her hand and was talking loudly to a bright-eyed woman in a cowboy hat who laughed at whatever his mother said.

Edgar spied Caroline sitting near the front with some boy. Was it possible? It looked like Jason Crumley. Was he everywhere, making Edgar's stomach tight? At least Caroline was talking to someone else, a girl beside

Crumley. And now here came Ceese walking toward Edgar's mother with a beer in his hand, but he wasn't alone. Victoria was with him. In this light it was clear she was younger than Edgar's mother, and taller. She was wearing rubber boots and an old shirt, and the air around her was very calm even in all the noise of dozens of conversations in the old wooden room getting ready for the show.

Victoria. She saw Edgar and waved to him, her face lit.

Then his mother was turning, her face lit too, to see Ceese. She embraced him too closely; she was ready for everything to be happy tonight. Then she noticed Victoria, and there was a quick and clumsy untangling, and a bit of beer spilled—just on the floor—and apologies and nervous laughter before his mother clasped Victoria's hand and her face shone, bright and hard.

Edgar was looking, not breathing.

"Are you Edgar?" someone said then. It was the red-haired woman in the cowboy hat, now suddenly beside him. He was standing apart, with people milling all around him. Probably he stuck out. "Stephanie has told me so much about you. I'm Lola!" she said.

Lola. Who owned the bar. Where his mother worked. "How are you enjoying Dawson so far?"

Edgar nodded. It was too loud to speak, wasn't it?

"We really love having your mother," Lola said. "She's a big hit already. Is she going to sing tonight?"

Edgar shook his head.

"How about you? Do you have the family pipes? I'm sure we could fit you in somewhere!"

Edgar shook his head again. Probably Lola could see his eyes widen in alarm. A seat opened up beside Caroline where the other girl used to be. Did he want to sit so close to Jason Crumley? Edgar started toward the front anyway. He hoped Lola wouldn't think him rude, just walking off. But then the girl came back and Edgar took a seat against the wall, looking sideways at the stage area.

He drew in his cheeks. He willed himself invisible in the shadows, out of the way.

His father. His father. What did he know of his father? His father had a leather case, the sort of thing a man might wear on a belt. It was straight on top and curved on the bottom and probably was made for holding a compass or something like that. Maybe Edgar's grandfather had owned it first, and he'd been the sort of man who worked in the woods and needed a compass. A woodsman? Who gave his son his brass compass or whatever it was, and now that instrument was gone. Only the leather case remained. Edgar's mother used it for holding her smaller earrings, which could get tangled together like fishing lures.

That was what Edgar could think about his father as he sat with his back to the wall watching the bands.

His father was not a drummer.

But Ceese was. He sat behind the lead singer, a man in a blue shirt with red suspenders that framed a large belly, and who grasped the microphone with both hands and sang with his eyes closed about a river, how everybody was alone in one. Edgar didn't think that he had heard the song before—he didn't know most songs—but it seemed like a good one. Ceese bounced in his seat and hit the metal discs sometimes—the cymbals—and smiled at the other players, a young man with a guitar and a girl with a fiddle.

Ceese looked like he could be both a father and a musician, and for the space of the song, Edgar imagined himself at home carefully taking out his mother's earrings and the like and then handing the leather case to Ceese and scanning his face to see if he recognized it.

It was a silly thought. Edgar knew it, but it was hard not to get carried away by the feeling of the music.

Did Edgar even want a father? Did he need one? He'd never had one, not even (as far as he knew) at the very beginning when he'd been too young to remember anyway.

Victoria joined the band for the next song. She hadn't changed at all but took the stage in her rubber boots. Whenever Edgar saw his mother perform, she always wore an extra shine, in her dress or hair, her jewelry. But Victoria looked shiny somehow even in her old clothes. Her voice glowed, and she seemed to be singing directly for Edgar even though her eyes covered all of the room.

"Someday this town will be my home.
Someday your love will be my own.
Someday."

It was hard, too, to keep from watching certain eyes—Ceese's as he knocked out the slow beat for her, and Victoria's as she sang, and Edgar's mother's as she stood on the other side of the room from where Edgar was sitting. She was leaning against the far wall, looking, looking.

At Ceese. Who stared at Victoria. Who met eyes with everyone else, it seemed, even Edgar, sitting almost invisibly in the shadows.

"Someday I'll walk with you.
Someday I'll know your heart is true.
Someday."

It was a slow song, but Victoria's voice filled the room. It made everyone sway even in their seats, and soon people were holding each other, dancing. Sometimes Edgar's mother danced by herself to the radio, and sometimes she pulled Edgar into shuffling along with her. Although, with many songs Edgar wasn't sure what he was supposed to be doing. If he had been sitting close to his mother now, she probably would have dragged him up to dance with her. . . .

Or maybe not.

His mother was staring hard at Victoria. She had one hand in her back pocket and one hand on her beer, and she wasn't even tapping her foot.

She looked like she couldn't wait for the song to be over.

She looked like she wanted to get up to sing herself.

When the song was over, when Victoria put the microphone back into its holder, Ceese kissed her onstage in front of everyone, and Edgar's mother dropped her beer bottle. It bounced on the wooden floor and didn't even break. Then she crossed to where Edgar was sitting and told him it was bedtime already, time to go, he had school tomorrow.

"You're going to have to get up by yourself because I'll be working late," she said. "Have you got your alarm clock?"

It was a strange question to ask him in the old ball-room while the next band was setting up. She knew he had a fold-up one that he kept in his small knapsack, the outside pocket, so that he wouldn't lose it.

She also knew he didn't have his real voice, his boy

voice, and so couldn't answer her at the moment.

"Come on. Let's go!" she said, and pulled him out of his chair far more roughly than if she had wanted him to dance.

One time on the radio, in the apartment before Roger's, the one that shook when the subway trains rumbled underneath them, Edgar had listened to a program about colors. What he remembered was that colors don't exist. That is, the white is not in the snowbank, the dark is not in the tree, the flush of his mother's face as they climbed the hill back home in the dying light was not really there. Those colors came out only in the mind of whoever was looking at them. It was a trick of the brain, as if a painter lived inside everyone's head and colored things according to how the person was seeing.

How was his mother seeing at the moment?

She had her head down. She was leaning into the hill. Maybe what she could glimpse of the night sky was blacker than what he could see.

Did she see any stars at all? Probably Victoria's voice darkened all those stars, shut them out completely.

If Edgar had had his voice, he probably would have said something like, "You knew there was a Victoria. He told us even before we met her."

Which was true. But maybe words don't exist either until they go through someone's brain. If they don't go through properly, they might mean nothing.

Edgar wasn't falling in love with Ceese. So he had heard the words clearly. From the start he had had a good idea what they might mean.

What might they mean?

Edgar felt the trouble coming on like a hard twist of rope inside him. His mother wouldn't give up now. She usually got a man she wanted. How did this work? Edgar had seen it, seen it before. . . .

Because Victoria had sung a beautiful song, Edgar's mother was more in love with Ceese than ever. She would not become tired like other people and look for someone else.

It's like a contest—a hockey game, or a big fight, he thought. *When she loses, it is only for a little while.*

BEAR

LATER, WHEN EDGAR TOOK BENJAMIN FOR A last walk before bed, he smelled bear. "Let's go have a look at him," Edgar said, but Benjamin held back, pretending he hadn't heard. "I've never seen a bear before," Edgar said. (The twisting rope was still inside him. He wanted to stretch it somehow, get free.)

"If he fills your nose already, why do you have to see him?" Benjamin replied.

Yes, why go chase a bear? A bear was scary. A bear was thrilling. Ceese was big and beautiful, a bit like a bear— for Edgar's mother, anyway. Why would his mother chase a bear who belonged with Victoria? His mother couldn't help herself. She liked the danger, the thrill of becoming close. So Edgar would chase a bear too. A real bear. So that he could understand what his mother was going to do—whatever it was—to steal Ceese from Victoria.

"We'll just get a little closer," Edgar said, pulling. The bear smelled stronger down the hill, toward the hospital, which was quiet and dark in parts, except for the entrance and some other lights.

Benjamin moved slightly with each tug, then settled to smell something interesting—someone's locked-up garbage, a rock peeking out of the ice, something else that used to be a fence post.

"Come on! Come on! It's too cold to wait around!" Edgar said. How was he ever to know? To feel like his mother, to understand how she wanted and what she craved?

Downhill. Edgar wasn't strong, but he could hurry, he could be urgent, he could annoy Benjamin into following him.

"It's all right. Leave the bear to make a little mess at night," Benjamin said. His tongue was hanging out and he was smiling like—what was the word Roger often used? A half-wit. But a clever one.

"I just want to see the bear," Edgar pleaded. They were all the way north in Dawson, living up against the bush. When else was he going to get his chance? His mother might decide at any moment to pack up again and go who knows where next.

And—what would happen after his mother wrestled Ceese from Victoria?

What would happen after they saw the bear?

They angled past the hospital to a darker space, a backyard of some sort in a town almost without backyards. But this was a large space with a snowy pathway leading across it—where the bear's paw prints stood out in the moonlight. Benjamin pulled back at the leash and stopped Edgar short.

"Close enough," the dog breathed.

"But I don't see him!"

How could he not? The bear smelled of a whole winter of stored-up farts, of a warm fridge rotting with food after the power has been turned off.

Of steel traps waiting to close, of hard teeth.

But Edgar couldn't see anything. The back of a big old building was now huddled in shadows. Gray clouds gripped a gloomy night sky.

Benjamin farted, and for a moment it was hard to tell the bear stench from Benjamin's gas.

If Edgar closed his eyes, if he put everything into the scent in the night air, into what his skin could feel in the crystal cold surrounding them . . .

There he was, Mr. Bear! Rooting in the bushes to their left, not far.

"Stay here," Benjamin growled softly.

Rooting in the bushes. What was in there?

"I hate the smell of him," Benjamin muttered.

The bear stopped rustling. Everyone stayed still, silently sniffing.

"Just makes trouble wherever he goes," Benjamin grumbled. "Why stand here breathing his filth?"

"In case it helps," Edgar whispered.

It was hard to tell how big the bear was, whether he was brown or black, how mean he might be. Benjamin wouldn't move a foot closer, so they stayed sniffing, listening.

"Only thing with trouble is staying clear," Benjamin said.

So Edgar dropped the leash and stepped closer. It was what his mother would do—what she did all the time. And Edgar was from her, so how was he to understand anything if he didn't take a step, or three, or ten, toward the black or brown stench in the shadows glaring at him?

"Hello, Mr. Bear," Edgar said.

The bear rumbled. Edgar could feel that in the ground, in his toes. But he kept walking closer.

"Get back here!" Benjamin snorted. "What—"

The bear got bigger the closer Edgar came. Was the bear Ceese, or his mother?

Or just a bear?

Edgar could see the rounded shoulders now. He could smell the bear so ready to pounce.

Those claws.

"Boy!" Benjamin said.

It was easy to get this far, but then Edgar's body was shaking; he could feel how close the bear was to running him over.

"Get back! Get back! Filthy fang crot!" Benjamin yelled, not at Edgar but at the bear. Then the black dog was past Edgar—moving faster than Edgar imagined possible—and barking right in front of the startled bear.

"Back! Back! Back!" Benjamin barked.

The bear yawned. For a moment Edgar could feel how close he was to raking his big paw across Benjamin's old face. But instead the bear shrugged, angled around, and snorted for the first several steps away. Then Edgar felt Benjamin's massive jaws on his coattail, and he was being dragged off.

"Stupid, stupid, stupid!" Benjamin snorted. "He bites through cans. What kind of treat you think your guts would be to him?"

"Yes," Edgar said, stumbling away.

"You could've been a smear on snow," Benjamin snarled.

Edgar's heart was boiling. Maybe that was what his

mother craved—leaning so close, smelling her own life nearly ripped open.

"You saved me," Edgar said finally as they were hurrying back up the hill.

"This time," Benjamin grumbled, like any one of those men—the Rogers, the Ceeses—hurrying so hard to save his mother from herself.

"You are very brave," Edgar said to Benjamin later that night. Edgar was lying awake in the dark, looking up at the strange ceiling, and Benjamin's form lay slumbering on his sleeping mat nearby.

Edgar didn't mind the big dog's smell anymore; he was getting used to it.

"You could have just let me keep walking. What do you think the bear would have done? He didn't seem so nasty. I wasn't going to hurt him."

Benjamin muttered something. He might've been dreaming.

"Or maybe," Edgar said, "I've already forgotten how scared I was. Have you met him before? Do you know that bear?"

Benjamin startled up for a second. Edgar could hear his jaws widening in a yawn. Finally Benjamin said, "The family's been in these parts long as me. Can't say I like bears."

"You were such a coward around Brottinger," Edgar said. "You rolled around and pretended to be so weak. Then with the bear—"

Benjamin burped. Edgar heard the dog's big tongue licking something. He leaned over and saw Benjamin twisted around, getting at his own abdomen. Finally Benjamin settled back down. Edgar closed his eyes and became himself again walking toward the bear. It wasn't cold, he wasn't afraid, the bear was not paying attention to him.

Edgar could stand there. He saw the bear much better in this version but could barely smell him. It was an odd thing to be in two different times at once. *Odd, and yet we do it all the time*, he thought. We walk toward the bear, and then later, when the bear is long gone, we walk toward him again and again.

The bear was Ceese. Ceese was large and strong. He looked friendly enough but probably could bite through cans if he had to. What did Ceese think he was doing, falling in love with Edgar's mother when he already had Victoria? Anybody would be in love with Victoria, the way she sang and wore those rubber boots.

What was happening right now at Lola's, where Edgar's mother was working the late shift? Was there music, was she singing, was Ceese there maybe with

Victoria, having a drink after the garage band competition? Had Victoria's band won?

Was everyone just going to pretend they weren't standing next to a disaster?

CHANGE

IN THE MORNING, QUIET. HIS MOTHER'S door was closed; the world seemed cool and calm. Edgar made the oatmeal, dressed himself, woke Benjamin and took him out on the back trail, the one behind Robert Service's cabin. Already the trail seemed familiar, as if Edgar had been walking it for years. On the bench not far along, where there was an opening in the trees and the town lay below them, quiet, just waking up, Edgar looked at the wide expanse of frozen river and the dark, dramatic hills behind. He'd brought his camera this time. He snapped a shot of the town.

"Everything looks peaceful," he said.

"When the ice breaks, you'll see the real river," Benjamin said.

"Isn't it the real river now?"

"It's real quiet."

Could Edgar speak normally today? Had his voice been returned to him? It was so hard to tell. When he talked to Benjamin, he sounded just like himself, not a dog at all, and Benjamin's barking, his woofs and grunts and whines and howls, all sounded like perfectly intelligible dog.

"Benjamin," Edgar said, "could you bark for me, really loud?"

"Why?" Benjamin sniffed.

"I want to hear it. Really loud."

When Benjamin gave it his full throat, when his whole body thundered, Edgar had to cover his ears. The snow shook, and the echo came back like a responding choir. "Edgar wants you to know it's me, Benjamin! Benjamin!" came the roar.

So Edgar pulled himself up and bellowed out—as much as it could be called a bellow—"And I am Edgar, Benjamin's friend. He saved me last night from the bear!"

Bear, bear, bear, came the echo.

It sounded like him completely.

When they got back to the house, Edgar's mother was still sleeping. There was no sign of anything that might or might not have happened in the night. Often Edgar didn't know when things were going to change drastically, when Roger was suddenly a danger, a man to flee, when they needed to quickly find a car, a train, or sleep on someone's floor. He paid attention but he didn't always know.

The days were changing noticeably, even since they had arrived. Though still early, it was brilliantly sunny now. The snow underfoot felt both solid and soft. There was still time before school started, but directly after the walk with Benjamin, Edgar left the house anyway. Depending on what had happened, his mother could be so sharp, a jagged edge that could cut blindly even after her coffee.

Heading down the hill, he turned left not right, away from the school but toward the highway and the dike, the river and the hills and the sun.

Would he be all right with his camera at school? He took shot after shot of the stretch of frozen white, the plunging slopes, and there, for the first time, a sliver of open water on the smaller river, the Klondike. It looked bluish-black in this light, and fast-flowing. Could things change so fast, just overnight?

Yes. Yes they could.

Ms. Lajoie was in a red-and-blue sweater today and had a soft scarf around her neck. She let Edgar keep his

camera in her desk, and she seemed happy still to let him
read quietly. He was not going to test his voice again, not
today. It seemed he was probably still a dog, or doglike.
When he read some more of "To Build a Fire," it was hard
not to think mostly about the dog whose master was being
so foolish:

> *The dog was sorry to leave and looked*
> *toward the fire. This man did not know cold.*
> *Possibly none of his ancestors had known*
> *cold, real cold. But the dog knew and all of*
> *its family knew. And it knew that it was*
> *not good to walk outside in such fearful cold.*
> *It was the time to lie in a hole in the snow*
> *and to wait for this awful cold to stop. There*
> *was no real bond between the dog and the*
> *man. The one was the slave of the other.*
> *The dog made no effort to indicate its fears*
> *to the man. It was not concerned with the*
> *well-being of the man. It was for its own*
> *sake that it looked toward the fire. But the*
> *man whistled, and spoke to it with the sound*
> *of the whip in his voice. So the dog started*
> *walking close to the man's heels and followed*
> *him along the trail.*

Edgar was not his mother's slave—at least he did not feel he was—but possibly, like the dog, he was trapped in a way in the life his mother was making for them. And he felt she was heading for disaster, just as the man walking away from the fire was sure to break through the frozen ice even though he was so confident. Later, when the worst had happened and the man was trying again desperately to light a fire:

> *After a time, he began to notice some feeling in his beaten fingers. The feeling grew stronger until it became very painful, but the man welcomed the pain. He pulled the mitten from his right hand and grasped the tree bark from his pocket. The bare fingers were quickly numb again. Next, he brought out his pack of matches. But the awful cold had already driven the life out of his fingers. In his effort to separate one match from the others, the whole pack fell in the snow. He tried to pick it out of the snow, but failed. The dead fingers could neither touch nor hold.*

Typically Edgar's mother *did* know when she had blundered . . . but only afterward, when everyone else knew too. She knew about her drinking and how bad she was with money. She knew everything that was wrong, and a lot of other things that weren't wrong. . . . She knew it all, as much as she believed in the moment that a Roger or a Ceese was going to change her life and everything would be so much better for herself and for Edgar.

He spoke to the dog, calling it to him. But in his voice was a strange note of fear that frightened the animal. It had never known the man to speak in such a tone before. Something was wrong and it sensed danger. It knew not what danger, but somewhere in its brain arose a fear of the man. It flattened its ears at the sound of the man's voice; its uneasy movements and the liftings of its feet became more noticeable. But it would not come to the man. He got down on his hands and knees and went toward the dog. But this unusual position again excited fear and the animal moved away.

Edgar had seen his mother on her knees, in a closet, her face a smear of teary mascara. He had smelled her breath, had cleaned up vomit in the bathroom and the bedroom and on the outside stairs. He had been like the dog in the story. Why shouldn't he be a dog now?

He knew what was coming.

He could smell it in the stillness of this town where they'd landed.

"How was school today?" his mother asked when he got home. She looked radiant in the kitchen, and for a moment it seemed clear she had forgotten about his barking, and so, too, Edgar almost forgot. He began to say, "All right. I read," but then just before the first sound, he knew he was still a dog-boy, that she would snap and all the beauty would drain from her face.

So he mumbled something instead. He pulled out his camera. He would capture her now. She had started singing something, a song about eyes lying. He got her reaching into the cupboard, and then turning to him with a can of soup in her hand. A strand of her hair across her face.

I see you, he thought. *I do see who you are.*

And it was not just her. It was her things—her purse by the stand near the door, with the mark in the leather where her hand always went. Her boots, pointed in odd directions, with their Toronto heels not right for Dawson snow and ice. Her sweater on the couch, still warm from where she'd been wrapped up in the afternoon sun, dreaming of what?

Of Ceese. Her life with him.

He could smell the man still, faintly, on her cloth-ing. Could that smell get into a photo, too? Would others know if they saw it?

She said suddenly, "What are you doing?" when he was pointing his camera at her lipstick on the side table near the big comfy chair. He froze and did not answer. She stared at him as if she knew exactly what he was doing.

What *was* he doing? He didn't know himself. Cap-turing these little bits of her, like portions of her scent he might read on the road somewhere.

She stared hard until he thought he'd crack into ice somehow.

Then finally she broke the spell. "Benjamin is stink-ing this place out. Could you take him for a walk, please?"

He would. He would. As far away as he could get.

KISS

THE *GEORGE BLACK*, IT TURNED OUT, WAS THE ferry used to cross the Yukon River in the warmer weather when the ice was out. Edgar found Caroline, and they brought Benjamin to see it. It was high on the riverbank down the road from the *Keno*, the big white paddle-wheel boat Edgar had tried to photograph the other day when he and his mother had bought groceries. The *George Black* was not wood like the *Keno*, but metal, orangey-red on the bottom and white on top, with room in the middle for cars and trucks.

Edgar took a picture of Caroline looking at it, as Benjamin sniffed at something strong around her feet. Alcohol, spilled some time ago?

"In the summer," Caroline said, "the ferry goes back and forth between here and West Dawson. You can hop on practically anytime. But when the ice breaks up, for a couple of weeks at least, maybe more, the river is too dangerous to cross, it's so high and full of ice. So there's no bridge and no ferry. If you live in West Dawson like Victoria, you're stuck. You need to stock up on groceries and everything."

In the late afternoon cold, the wind was slight but still felt raw on Edgar's cheeks. And Caroline was looking around as she talked, as if maybe the ice might go out right at that moment. From where they were standing, a black triangle of open water stretched even longer than before in the middle of the river. The orange marker with the wire tied to shore looked lonely and cold out on the ice, and not very far at all from the black open stretch.

"Sometimes families will move to Dawson for the breakup. They'll stay at the Eldorado or with friends and it'll be a big party. Victoria normally comes to stay with us, and she gets a friend to look after her dogs. But sometimes breakup happens so fast, you get stuck. There isn't time to pack and head on over."

Benjamin said, "Victoria has the warmest fires." He was sniffing, sniffing. Then he growled, "Rot crap!"

Brottinger appeared suddenly, coming down the road from the dog park, with Jason Crumley holding his leash taut.

"What, you brought a whole audience?" Jason called out to Caroline, who blushed fiercely.

"I didn't come here to see you!" she snapped.

"No, no. You're just hanging out by the *George Black* looking at the beautiful snow!"

Brottinger did not seem to be in a barking mood. He sniffed Benjamin, who stood still, head lowered. Then Brottinger grumbled to Edgar, "You still here, Meat Boy?"

Benjamin smiled sickly, then said, "Not for long, no. We're just going. Great to see you!" And he started away, pulling Edgar, who was holding the leash, with him.

But Caroline stayed where she was. "Don't know what you think you're going to do here out in the open where everyone can see," she said to Jason.

"If I'd known you were coming, I would've brought a bottle," Jason replied, grinning.

"You don't have a bottle, and I wouldn't drink from it anyway." Caroline kicked a chunk of ice. Benjamin stood with Edgar some distance off, the dog's head down still, like a servant who is not supposed to be listening.

Edgar fingered his camera. He thought, *If I were brave or something, I'd catch that look on Jason's twisted face.* But Edgar didn't move. He didn't dare.

"That's fine." Jason was standing too close now, too

close. Caroline didn't turn aside, but she wasn't completely looking at Jason either. Edgar had seen his mother stand just the same way, and pull men in, closer and closer, without seeming to do anything.

Jason tilted his head toward her.

Benjamin started to growl, softly at first. Jason didn't stop. And Caroline wasn't pulling away either.

Then something thunderous rumbled from Benjamin's throat. Brottinger sprang at him, but Benjamin didn't flinch. The two dogs circled and snarled, Benjamin taller and louder, his teeth suddenly barred like weapons.

Edgar didn't know whether to drop the leash or pull hard, so he just stood, frozen.

"Benjamin, hey! Benjamin!" Caroline yelled, and came to intervene even though the two dogs sounded like the start of World War Three.

"Brot! Here, boy! Now!" Jason yelled.

Benjamin's lips were curled. He'd puffed himself to look twice the size of Brottinger.

They pulled the dogs apart. No one got bitten or slashed by claws. There was no blood on anyone's neck.

"I wasn't going to kiss him!" Caroline said when they were walking away.

"Yeah, yeah, yeah," Benjamin huffed.

"I just wanted to see if he really would show up."

Caroline fondled Benjamin's ears through her mittens. "But you defended me, my gentle beast!"

"Uh-huh," Benjamin groaned. "Why does everybody around here want to smell the bear up close?"

In Edgar's room Caroline turned her bright eyes fully upon him. "I'm not crazy about Jason Crumley," she said. "I'm not that stupid. But how am I supposed to learn about anything, with the boys around here?"

She was sitting cross-legged on his bed. Benjamin, lying on his mat on the floor, munched some biscuits Caroline had fetched him for defending her.

"How am I even going to learn how to kiss somebody if the only option in this whole town is Jason Crumley?"

It was hard to avoid her gaze. In a different way she was doing her silent trick, pulling Edgar in, almost with an invisible string.

He did like looking at her.

Did she want to kiss *him* now?

Did he—

"It's just practice," she said. "I think you're practically like my brother. And you're not as young as you've been letting on, are you?" Edgar blinked. Blinked. How had she guessed? "It's all right. I won't spill your secret." She leaned closer to him. "Let's try this out. So later on we'll know what we're supposed to do."

The door was closed. Edgar wasn't trying to move, but somehow he was on the bed now too, sitting opposite her.

"I think . . . Let's try immobilizing the target," she said, and held his face by the cheeks. "Close your eyes maybe. Just . . . tilt."

If he relaxed, if he just did what she—

Her lips were wet. They swiped against his, and then she pulled away.

"You have to open a little bit. No licking, though," she said.

He let her move his face this way and that.

"Did you brush your teeth at lunchtime?" Caroline asked. Edgar nodded, he had. "Me too," she said, and they practiced some more.

"Close your eyes. Pretend you're enjoying it," she said after a time.

He was, somewhat. Her lips were warm. Her cheek felt very soft against his, and when she bit his lip, it was only a little, nothing terrible.

Finally she pulled back. "You're all hot in the face," she said.

So was she. Her ears, especially, seemed to be burning.

"We don't need to tell anybody about all this. Especially not Jason Crumley. This is just for practice, understand?"

Edgar nodded as if he did.

Caroline hopped off the bed. It had been easy to

forget, for a while, about the trouble brewing with Edgar's mother and Ceese, who probably weren't just practicing, not at all.

Edgar opened his mouth to tell her. "I'm worried—" he began to say, but even he could hear the whiny sharp barks that continued to capture his voice.

"Guess there's no fear of you telling anyone but Benjamin!" Caroline said on her way out.

That night, in Edgar's dreams a bear thundered out of the woods on the trail by the bench where Edgar was sitting, trying to stay quiet. He was a greasy black bundle of spiky fur, and Edgar couldn't move because there was so little room on the bench. As the bear crowded in, Edgar shrank and shrank, but where else to go? He was already on the edge, deep inside the woods.

The bear snuffled at him, pressed; the bear's snout was hot and wet and smelled like sulfur matches just as they are lighting. Edgar wanted to hit back, to call out, to run, but he was so small. What could he do? The bear was at his neck, on his face, his lips, licking hard, slobbering.

"Just get off! Get off! Get, get!" Edgar said, but not in his voice. He sounded as if a gerbil or chipmunk were inside him doing the talking.

Edgar turned his back. He held his head and scrunched down, but where could he go—where?

He awoke in a sweat, and the stink of Benjamin lying on the mat beside his bed made him hold his nose as he got up and walked along the cold floor to the bathroom. He left the lights off. After a minute it wasn't so black. He could see himself in shades of gray in the mirror. His pajamas were rumpled. His hair looked like a bear *had* been licking and flattening it.

He walked into the kitchen. By the dull light of the stove clock, he looked again at the old map of Dawson taped up on the fridge. There was the squiggle of the Yukon River, and there was West Dawson, and there was the word: "Abandoned."

Maybe it had been abandoned long ago, but Victoria was there now, and she had dogs. Hadn't Ceese told him the story of Rupert and how the wolves had tried to lure him out of his little shed?

Looking out the back window, squinting into the darkness, Edgar felt sure he could see the smudge in the hills where West Dawson must be. And he could feel it, just a bit, that some of those kisses from Caroline had not been just practice. They'd done something to his scared and worried parts down in the blood of his quietest insides.

ISAAC

BREAKFAST. EDGAR GOT UP ALONE AS USUAL
and fixed the porridge. His mother had left him a note
with twenty-five dollars to buy milk and bread and boxed
macaroni with powdered cheese on his way home for
lunch. She was sleeping now, of course. Edgar had no
idea what might or might not have happened in the night.
A cupboard was open; there were crumbs on the counter
where she had had toast after her shift. Yet another beer
bottle. By the front door her boots were splayed as usual,
and her coat sat on the floor where she had dropped it
from her body upon entering. Edgar had seen her do it a
hundred times, how she got through the door at home—
wherever home was lately—and started shedding layers as
if getting rid of the day or night left behind.

He found his camera. He knew he shouldn't, but he

took more pictures. He could smell something strong on her things, something of what had happened when she'd been out there in the world.

It was harder than usual to rouse Benjamin for his walk, and he seemed reluctant to climb the hill leading to the trail behind Robert Service's log cabin. When they got to the lookout, Edgar said, "Are you sick, Benjamin?"

He seemed even stinkier than usual and was moving stiffly.

Benjamin said, "Mornings are hard when you're big and old as me."

Edgar thought, *If he sits down here, I would never be able to move him on my own. I'd have to go get Caroline, and even then we'd still have trouble.*

Benjamin was standing still, head down, not looking at all at the town below them slowly waking.

Edgar said, "Were they real kisses?" He meant the ones from Caroline. Benjamin had been there after all, on his mat. Maybe he knew?

"Real enough to pay attention," Benjamin grunted, and then he started back on his own, pulling Edgar behind him.

There was a new display now at the library. Edgar was drawn to it as soon as he walked in during the period of free reading Ms. Lajoie allowed him that morning. The first thing he saw was a picture of Chief Isaac on a stand by the window, above a table with books and display cards. Isaac had three white feathers sticking out of a black hat, and a gray mustache, and was wearing beads or at least a colorful band across his chest, and he seemed to be looking at Edgar but also past him too, to something else beyond.

The display was about the Tr'ondëk Hwëch'in, the Hän-speaking people who had been in the area when all the miners and others had arrived. Edgar remembered how Ceese had called those miners swarming mosquitoes, and here was a black-and-white picture of the main street of Dawson flooded with them, white men crowding even the roofs of the buildings to see something down on the main street. Ceese had said that to survive, Chief Isaac had moved his people down the river to Moosehide to live on their own in their own way.

Here was a printed card with a quote from Chief Isaac in December 1911: *White man come and take all my gold. Take millions, take more hundreds fifty millions, and blow 'em in Seattle. Now Moosehide Injun want Christmas. Game is gone. White man kills all moose and caribou near Dawson, which is owned by Moosehide. Injun everywhere have own hunting grounds. Moosehides hunt up Klondike, up Sixtymile, up Twentymile, but game is all gone. White man kill all.*

Edgar opened a book with Chief Isaac on the cover, *Hammerstones*, to a page about a powerful dancing stick, the *gänhäk*, that Chief Isaac brought to Alaskan tribes when he realized the worst was happening to his people. Chief Isaac stayed long enough to teach the dances and songs, knowing his own people could not keep them, with such a mosquito problem back home. But it wasn't just mosquitoes—his people were starving. The moose and caribou and fish had been food. And those songs and dances were all their history, their stories going back forever.

Edgar's fingers were trembling as he read the book. He felt some of the ache of the loss even though it had happened long ago and not to him. The picture of Chief Isaac was a blur of colors, a dance of blues and greens and browns in the background, perhaps a forest behind his hat and face, a forest and mountains, and a slashing red on each arm by the bottom of the picture, a white shawl over his shoulders. Edgar took his own picture of it so that he could remember better the strong face and the colors and some of the ache.

And then Edgar read a little paragraph about how now, generations later, even though the Tr'ondëk Hwëch'in did not live anymore in Moosehide (*abandoned*), the songs and the dances were coming back to them from the Alaskan tribes who'd kept them, kept their promise. The Tr'ondëk Hwëch'in were relearning their heritage because Chief Isaac had thought and planned ahead and had found a safe place and helpful people.

He'd known what he was about, Chief Isaac. Edgar could feel that somehow—just looking at the painting, reading these words on paper from years and years ago.

PEABODY'S

AT LUNCHTIME EDGAR REMEMBERED HIS mother's money and the instructions to buy bread and milk and boxed macaroni. But on the way home his feet did not take him directly to the General Store. He went instead to Peabody's Photo Parlour and stood outside the window fingering his camera. There were old-time photographs of miners and fancy ladies. Or maybe they were modern people dressed up to be old-time. He knew he could buy nothing there—and anyway the money in his pocket was for food, not anything to do with pictures.

It was cold standing outside, so he pulled open the door and walked into an empty shop—or at least no one was behind the counter. A rack had pictures and cards of ravens and Klondike miners, steamboats and Mounties and ladies in full dresses standing outside log shacks on muddy paths instead of roads.

"Edgar!" came a voice, and Victoria walked out from behind a curtain in the back. She was wearing a warm red scarf and a dark green sweater, and her eyes drank him in tenderly. "What are you doing here?"

What a relief to see her! He remembered the sad and beautiful song, the stillness until his mother had stormed out.

He didn't want to bark, so he lifted his camera until Victoria took it off his shoulder.

"Very nice! Do you need some pictures developed?"

He looked at her, helpless.

"You're not shy around me, are you?" She bent down to look him in the eye. "Caroline has a good time showing you around. She's full of stories of what you guys get up to with Benjamin."

Edgar found a piece of paper on the counter and borrowed a pen. *I can't pay you*, he wrote. *I have to buy milk and bread and macaroni.*

After she had read the note, she touched his cheek. "Let's see what you've got in here anyway."

She found a cord that connected his camera to a large machine, and soon enough the pictures he'd taken showed up on-screen. She was quiet, looking at the angry boy on the plane and Edgar's mother's hairdryer peeking out of her exploded luggage, and the shots Edgar had taken on the river and looking up at the Moosehide Slide and other places. When she saw the photos of his mother, and of her things, she said, "You have an eye, Edgar. Pretty quirky, your way of looking at the world." She was gazing deeply at him. "What are these about?" she asked gently.

She meant the lipstick, the handbag, the sweater, all the things that smelled of his mother.

What could he write? What?

He showed again the note. *I can't pay you. I have to buy milk and bread and macaroni.*

She smiled; she eyed him again; she was figuring it out. Finally she said, "All right. One time. But I don't own this place—you're going to owe me. You tell me which ones."

It was simple, actually. Victoria was generous. Edgar hadn't taken all that many photos, but she made copies, and he left them in ordinary places: at the base of telephone poles, near the corners of quiet buildings, by posts and trees and on the side of old structures where countless dogs had already marked. What was one more little bit of news?

Chief Isaac, of course, people would recognize. This was his land, his people's hunting and fishing grounds. And Edgar's mother's things—maybe no one would notice. Or they wouldn't care what they were looking at.

Forget the eyes a moment—smell goes straight to what a body knows for itself. That was something Edgar was starting to know, being part dog. How much smell would leak from a photo anyway? Maybe nothing.

He was just feeling his way, feeling. Maybe, if he left enough traces of his mother, if he told her story in these little bits, people would begin to know about her, and it wouldn't matter if she couldn't stop herself.

Someone else would. They would know about her, somehow, from all these little clues, the way the dogs in town know who's sick and who's strong and who has to jump like a crazy skurd to pee that high on a community pole.

A woman in thick boots watched him from the other side of the street, standing in front of the Westminster Hotel, a tired pink building with a sign that said ROMANCE CAPITAL OF THE YUKON. She looked tired herself; a cigarette drooped from her lips. Some friends joined her to smoke in a circle and to watch as Edgar left his photos here and there. When he reached the corner, he looked back and saw that the woman had crossed the street to pick up one of the pictures and peer at it intently.

Could she smell anything? Did she know? How could this be any way to spread the news, or stop it? And what was the news, anyway?

A new woman was in town who couldn't help herself, she was going to blow up lives she hardly even knew.

Just time to go to the grocery store, and then, as he headed up the hill for a bite of lunch, who was there to meet him but Dr. Gumstul. She was out walking her own dog, a young husky who thrust his nose inside Edgar's jacket and very much wanted him to drop the bag of groceries he was carrying.

"Edgar—hello!" Dr. Gumstul said. "How are you feeling? Is your throat any better?"

It was an odd thing to say. Friendly enough, Edgar supposed. Had she really forgotten that Edgar's throat wasn't sore at all? Or was she just giving Edgar a chance to talk, if he could?

He shook his head in answer to the question and everything else.

"I've heard from that specialist in Whitehorse that I told you about," Dr. Gumstul said. "She'll be in town next month, so I'd like to make an appointment. I'll be in touch with your mother about it, all right?"

Edgar tried to smile in a reassuring way. But really—who knew where they were going to be next month? Everything could come unraveled over a weekend.

The doctor finally let him go, and he hurried farther

up the hill, realizing that lunchtime was pretty well over by now. But his mother would be worried about the groceries if he didn't bring them right away.

At the top of Eighth Avenue he looked down the hill to see Dr. Gumstul in the distance holding back her dog, bending down to pick up something, a picture maybe, blowing in the slight breeze.

COLLAR

A FEW MINUTES THEN FOR LUNCH. HE GAVE his mother the change from the groceries. What questions could she ask, when all he could do was bark and she hated reading his explanations? He barely had time to wolf down a peanut butter and banana sandwich before turning around and hurrying back to school.

No need to mention the doctor, or the pictures, or how beautiful and warm Victoria had been, and kind to him in the photo shop, developing those pictures when he had no money to pay.

Why did the world not slow down for a boy with so much to think about already because of what had just happened in the last few days, the last hours even? There was Edgar's mother, of course, and Ceese and Victoria, the band competition and the other competition, and whatever was happening at the bar at night, because something must be happening, knowing his mother, her nature, what she probably went ahead and did.

And not only that—the bear, and Edgar's voice, and Jason Crumley and Brottinger and kissing practice with Caroline, and now the whole long story of Chief Isaac and his people, the Tr'ondëk Hwëch'in. It was a difficult name that Ms. Lajoie wrote out on the whiteboard because of the new library exhibit, and everyone else seemed to know anyway. This whole band of people who'd been here already when all those savage, desperate gold rushers had arrived by the tens of thousands with their tons of equipment. Shovels and picks and tents, and tinned biscuits, and how they had all hoped to just pick chunks of gold right out of the creeks and rivers where the Tr'ondëk Hwëch'in fished already. And the whole place had been a moose swamp before it was a town.

Gold-rushing mosquitoes.

All that to think about, and now Edgar's pictures and Chief Isaac littering the streets because it had just felt like the right thing to do. . . . Edgar wanted an hour or eight or maybe even a few weeks to go away by himself, or perhaps with Benjamin, and think it all through. What it meant. What he thought of this landslide of thinkables he had to deal with.

(Thinkables. Maybe that was a word.)

But the world did not stop. Recess happened, and even a sunny corner away from everyone else did not stay quiet. Jason Crumley found a leash someone had left clipped to the school fence—a chewed black nylon cord with a collar dangling on the end—and would not leave it alone. He unclipped it. He whipped it at his friends, other boys around him. He looked around and saw Edgar watching him.

"Hey! Hey! Hey, dog-boy!"

Why couldn't the world shut up for a week, for a moment even?

Edgar pulled back his cheeks; he stayed still. He imagined himself wearing Chief Isaac's hat, smoking a pipe, looking right at and yet over the heads of those around him.

"Hey, dog-boy!" Crumley yelled, and snapped the leash.

It was not a big schoolyard. It did not take long before the leash was snapping close to Edgar's feet.

"Bark for me, dog-boy! I know you can do it. Woof! Woof!"

How quickly the collar was around Edgar's neck. He didn't even get his fingers in the way. And then he had to move. Crumley jerked him, and his head snapped back.

"You want to be a dog, let's treat you like a dog!"

Edgar was falling now. He tried to brace himself, but he couldn't breathe and the ground spun hard—

"Hey! Hey!" someone else called. It sounded like—

And then there was a lot of yelling and fighting. Edgar couldn't see much. People were around him, and Caroline was the one who loosened the collar so that he could breathe again. She said, "What are you doing, Edgar! Why'd you let him noose up your neck like that?"

And there were teachers, too, and it got serious: soon enough they were in the principal's office, and even Edgar's mother was there with Ceese, arguing with Jason and his mother. Edgar's mother wanted Jason out of school for the rest of his life practically, and the principal looked like he wished the law allowed him to beat the boy half to death, but Jason said he'd put the leash on Edgar only because he was acting like a dog anyway, and had threatened to bite him the other day for no good reason at all. And the way he said it—like he was fiddling a tune, like you had to tap your foot—even Edgar started to believe that maybe he deserved a collar around his neck for being so doggish.

The way Jason defended himself in the principal's office made everyone lose their voice for a moment. They'd been like a big arguing choir, all singing at once, but after the fiddler was through, it was quiet and everyone turned to Edgar to see was he really doggish or not?

Jason said, "He can't even speak. All he does is bark!"

So they were all looking at where Edgar was sitting. His throat was tight anyway. He felt like the collar had left a big red band around his neck.

"Sweetie, just say a few words," Edgar's mother said in a frightened way. He knew she didn't actually believe he could.

They were all looking at him, even Ms. Lajoie, who was lovely in a different scarf today, a blue one, and who had yelled at Jason because she knew already he could be a bully. She said what did it matter if the boy was barking?

But with Edgar's mother there, who could hear her?

His mother said, her voice trembling, "Just tell us, Edgar, how the collar got around your neck. How he put it there."

There was no way to disappear with all those eyes burning at him.

Edgar said, "Woof! Woof-woof, woof-woof!"

He was thinking, *When I try to speak human, I sound to everyone like I am barking, so I'll bark and—*

It just sounded like barking.

In a few minutes Edgar's mother was pulling him home by the scruff of his jacket.

I'm sorry. I'm sorry. For all the trouble I'm causing, Edgar wrote in his notebook and passed it over to his mother. They were sitting at the kitchen table. She had opened a bottle of beer and was drinking it in front of him in the middle of the day.

"I just don't understand," she said. "I needed you to be normal at least for a few days. This is, like, my last chance, don't you see? I don't want to screw this up!"

The beer smelled like poison to him, like the cardboard bed on the subway grating that he wasn't supposed to look at when they passed by.

"You know? You know? I've had a lot of bad luck in my life. A person can take so much of it, and then she can't. I just needed you to be able to go to school and blend in and be quiet. Like you do. What's different here? Is it the dog? Is it Benjamin? Is he too much to take care of?"

Why are you making Ceese the new Roger? Edgar wrote, and passed the notebook to her.

"What? What?" She picked up her beer as if she might club him with it, so he winced. He couldn't help himself. "Oh, don't be such a baby! There is no new Roger! Where did you come from, saying things like that? Is that why you're barking?"

She could not stay seated. She got up almost like the angry bear and paced in front of the kitchen window.

I do not know why I am barking, he wrote.

She shoved the bottle into the sink. He thought it would break, but instead it tipped over and stinky beer oozed down the drain.

"The bigger question is—Edgar, honestly, you know I love you, but—where the hell did you come from? How are you even my child? I don't know half of what you're saying to me, and I'm not talking about when you're barking. *Is Ceese the new Roger?* What do you mean by that?"

Edgar made his eyes large.

"You're my kid. You're too young. I can't be talking to you about these kinds of—"

I smelled you both, he wrote.

Her jaw worked up and down several times, but nothing came out. Finally: "So what, now you're like my dog who smells every scrap of private business that goes on in my life? There are limits, Edgar! You're not supposed to know about any of this stuff. Be a kid! Go to school, play baseball, just be normal!"

She paced. She thrust her hands into her hair. Her eyes were red with tears about to spill.

Edgar wrote: *There is still snow. It's too cold for baseball.*

She slapped the counter. "You're joking about this?"

Benjamin came up the stairs, slowly, to see what was going on. He sniffed, sniffed at Edgar and his mother.

"What's he smelling? What's he smelling?" Edgar's mother said. "Well, I didn't even finish one beer. How's that? Promise me you're not ganging up on me."

In a moment it was going to be hard to breathe, they would not be able to continue. She was his mother—that did mean something—but his fingers were aching and he could hear his heart in his eardrums. She was looking at him so hard, he had to focus on the pad before him.

Ceese has his Victoria. That's all that is wrong with him. Otherwise he would be fine as the new Roger.

He had written it but was afraid to show her. He couldn't move his hand away, until finally she said, "Oh, for God's sake!" and ripped the pad from him.

She looked, she looked. She seemed about to hit him over the head with the pad. Instead she leaned close to him, she gripped him by the shoulders too hard for it to be a hug. "Look at me, look at me," she whispered harshly until he had to show her his eyes. "There is no new Roger. Do you understand?"

He didn't. He didn't understand her at all.

Finally she let him go. She hurried to her room. The bang of the door rattled the cups in the cupboard in the kitchen, where Edgar still sat. It jangled his spine through the chair.

LIGHT

SILENCE, SILENCE. LATE IN THE AFTERNOON they walked across the highway—which was still empty of cars—out where the two rivers met. Then they descended the steep bank and headed along what looked like a snow-mobile trail, although there were traces of ski tracks and footprints as well. Benjamin was slow but uncomplaining, and Edgar dawdled behind his mother to take photographs from a safe distance. The snow was firm underfoot, shiny, although there were deep cracks sometimes in the ice. The light shone off humps in the river, as if waves had been frozen in place. Is that how it happened, the river had frozen in a moment? Like his mother now, frozen because of what he had said on a pad of paper.

Maybe not. The river was unfreezing now, even as they were walking, although everywhere around them the ice still seemed thick. Stretches of water had opened in places, near the shore and over there where an island poked itself between the two rivers.

Ice, snow, hills, river. Trees, rock, sky, sun. Edgar could feel himself a tiny spot in the silent collision of what?

It wasn't just his mother's anger. It was like the whole world piling mountains against him.

Benjamin said, "Haven't been out here in a long time."

They were on the main river now, the Yukon, heading away from town. Dawson was gone, practically, a blur of colors under the Moosehide Slide.

Edgar had frozen the words inside her. And all he could do was bark. What he'd written had been too true to be helpful.

Even mosquitoes would have to be quiet in the winter, Edgar thought.

They were heading toward a bend, but it was so far away, Edgar didn't think they would reach it. It was like the morning of their arrival, when they had started off walking from the airport.

He took a picture of the speck of his mother walking away from him in the distance. Hills, sky, trees, snow, ice, all enormous around her.

Benjamin said, "Soon now, all this will break up. A whole different river then."

"Different how?" Edgar asked.

"Nobody walking on a river this wild."

Edgar's mother was sitting by the shore in the shadows, smoking, her legs crossed. Edgar could smell the cigarette long before he could see the expression in her eyes— distant, like she was looking across an ocean at something no one else could see. When Edgar and Benjamin got to her, she said, "Now, if I was a good mother, I would have brought a picnic, a thermos with hot chocolate. And if I was a Girl Guide, I'd make a little fire, and you could roast marshmallows and feed some to the dog, and then later, when you're all grown up and speaking at my funeral to the three other people who show up, you'd say, 'She wasn't such a bad mother. Sometimes we did fun things, and she thought of other people sometimes.'"

The cigarette smoke smelled foul from such close range even though they were outside. There was no wind, and Edgar felt hot still from the long walk.

"Sometimes you ask me about your father, but, you know, it's your grandfather I should be telling you about. He's the one who warped me. It's his fault." She sucked in, sucked in, then blew out enormously and stubbed out the cigarette.

"I know. It's disgusting," she said. "I can tell by the

expression on your face. This is my very last one." She pulled the package from her coat pocket. "I'd leave the rest here, but I don't want to be accused of littering. You already think I'm an adulterer or something."

Benjamin was standing patiently. Possibly he did not lie down so that he could avoid having to get up again. Had they brought him too far?

"Daddy was a money guy. He always wore a three-piece suit. He had schemes, land deals, shopping centers, apartment buildings. Sometimes we lived in huge houses in Rosedale, and sometimes it was a rental in Scarborough where the toilet never got fixed. At least twice we lost all our furniture. I swear it was the same guys in the same truck from the same company who showed up to haul everything away. I went to three different private schools, and I think there's still outstanding debt beside my name, probably at all of them. Daddy had girls, too. I won't call them women. I remember walking down Yonge Street once when I was a teenager. I was skipping classes, and Daddy was skipping out with some girl who looked like a hooker, heels to here and a dress not much longer than a T-shirt. He never saw me, though I walked by him, practically stuck my tongue out. And one time when I took up with a so-called banker friend of his—well, I won't tell you about that, not my finest hour. Daddy blew a gasket over that when he found out. It was like—'Well, he's no better than I am!' which was somewhat the point."

All the time she was talking, she was still looking at the horizon, at ghosts far, far off. But now she steadied her gaze at Edgar. "You see me. You've seen me at my worst. You've seen me more or less getting through. I'm sorry. I probably should have just given you up for adoption, but how could I, when you came out, with those big dark eyes like you knew everything already? I'm sorry I'm a screwup, but you know, I read somewhere that maybe we choose our parents, maybe it's our own fault what family we get born into." She drilled her eyes into him. "You know my daddy's middle name was Edgar, don't you?"

He hadn't known that. His grandfather had died before Edgar was born.

"Yeah, well, I wanted him, from his seat in hell, to understand that I at least could grow someone worthy of who he might have been. And here you are. My gift to the world." She looked around at all the ice and snow like she really wanted a drink.

Edgar shifted. It was hard to know what to say. Finally she rubbed her legs. "I was too hot when I sat down, but now I'm cooling off. Did you get some good pictures?"

Edgar took one then of her looking at him, full of this strange moment, and he showed her. The screen was dull in the daylight, but even so she liked his shots of the sun glinting off the ice and snow, of Dawson huddled in the distance, of Benjamin black against the silvery light. The one of her—well, she said her hair wasn't right.

But she gave him a hug anyway; she crushed him within an inch of being able to breathe. "If I hadn't had you, I'd probably be in my grave by now," she choked out, and her tears flooded, almost unbearably, in warm wet sobs against his cheek.

They got cold, they turned to leave, and then they were heading back across the frozen Yukon, the light hitting the hills to fill his eyes, to flush him with a strange vibration. (The hills themselves suddenly seemed to be both black and white as before, snow and ice dotted with trees and rocks, but also bathed in gold—trembling, hand-painted.) Benjamin stopped too. Who knew what he could see? Maybe he smelled the soak of it, the tremble. Maybe to him it was an orchestra blast or like lying down in a shaded meadow of soft grass.

Edgar's body felt full of gold somehow—not the metal but the sense, the throb of it. Clean air, pure light, a whole rugged landscape suddenly showing itself, like an enormous moon emerging from behind a wall of clouds.

Those hills had been there all along. He'd taken pictures. He'd already appreciated the way they looked.

But this was like breathing for the first time.

(Was it because his mother loved him? She truly did in her broken way, and so surely all the wrong things happening were going to be all right?)

This was like opening his eyes.

"Edgar!" his mother called. She was far away again, looking back at him. "What are you doing? Hurry up! I'm freezing!"

He was looking. Just looking. With his whole self.

He raised his camera and knew he was not going to capture it, not a fraction of it. He couldn't describe it at all.

"Edgar!"

Already the light was changing. He would have to move. He had the feeling he was going to remember this moment inside his body somehow.

Remember what?

The prick of his toes in his boots getting cold.

The sense of his grandfather, a man Edgar had never even seen a picture of but whose name he shared, smiling hard at the world he wanted to charm.

His mother's smoke.

Benjamin still, true, silent.

And those hills plunging down to the frozen river, now with fingers of gold—the sense of how light never stayed the same—filling him, filling him.

With what?

LOVE

MS. LAJOIE WAS WAITING AT THE HOUSE when they got back, leaning against their front door, reading a book. How long had she been there? Her cheeks did not seem overly red. She seemed perfectly contented in her parka, in her fur-and-leather boots that disappeared beneath the hem of her long coat. "I was hoping we could get a chance to talk, the three of us," she said.

"What, you don't think Benjamin should be part of this meeting?" Edgar's mother said.

Ms. Lajoie actually looked down at the dog as if Edgar's mother might have been serious. But Benjamin was exhausted, barely standing after being out too long. What was he going to say, anyway? *No tragedy, barking like a dog*"?

"Come on in. We're freezing!" Edgar's mother said.

Edgar took Benjamin downstairs and waited as the old dog circled, circled, then lay down. He didn't seem too cold, just ready to close his eyes. Maybe he would dream of the light on those hills, of whatever it was that filled a body.

Upstairs again, in the kitchen with tea water on the boil, Ms. Lajoie said, "I am so, so sorry for what happened today. I don't know how Jason got hold of a dog collar. It should never have ended up around Edgar's neck. And Edgar should never have been subjected to so much pressure in the principal's office to speak and to be a certain way. Please accept my apologies on behalf of the school and the whole community." Her eyes levered between Edgar's and his mother's. His mother's face was pale, blank.

Finally his mother said, "Edgar never has mixed well on the playground, and sometimes he doesn't fit in just because of who he is. I know he's not normal." She shifted her gaze to Edgar. "You've got me for a mom, for one. That's a huge handicap right there. It's a wonder you didn't start barking right out of the gate."

Edgar's mother poured tea for Ms. Lajoie and herself, and mixed hot chocolate for Edgar, making a show, it seemed to Edgar, of being a mother. Ms. Lajoie blew on her mug and leaned across the table toward Edgar. "So you haven't always had this problem, Edgar?"

"Good God, no!" Edgar's mother said. "He was fine when we were in Toronto. It's only since we got here. But I haven't been able to provide much stability. We came here to start over. There were some issues—"

Ms. Lajoie stayed quiet, but Edgar's mother didn't say anything more. The pad and pen were right there still on the table in front of Edgar. She was going to ask him—

"What can I do, Edgar, to make you feel safe and comfortable in the classroom?" Ms. Lajoie asked.

If he waited—

"He's never had this trouble before," Edgar's mother said again. "But elsewhere, other things. He's just not normal. Are you, Edgar?" She smiled in her too-bright way. "Normal doesn't work in our family. But other teachers have just let him read in the back of the class. There's a word—what am I looking for, Edgar?" She bumped the pad closer to him.

Autodidact, Edgar wrote.

"That's it. He teaches himself. You could test him if you want. He's off the charts for some things. I read to him way too much when he was too young to protest, I guess. Do you remember, Edgar, all the reading we did together?"

He remembered the sting of her cigarette smoke when he sat on her knee, the loveliness of her voice, the colors on the page when there were pictures.

"I remember when he was in grade four, he was supposed to do a project on—what was it, Edgar? Water, I think. Properties and what it's used for. Instead you wrote this whole philosophical thing—"

Ms. Lajoie kept switching her dark, lovely eyes between Edgar and his mother. Her skin smelled sharp all of a sudden, as if—

"What grade is Edgar supposed to be in?" Ms. Lajoie asked.

As if her blood had picked up an electric current of doubt.

"Technically grade six," Edgar's mother said. "But in Toronto he was working in the seven–eight curriculum."

Both women now were looking too hard at Edgar.

"What grade did you tell them, Edgar?" his mother asked finally.

Edgar felt his shoulders shrugging.

"I teach grade four," Ms. Lajoie said.

"Physically, I know," Edgar's mother said, "he looks a lot younger. But he'll be twelve this summer."

Both women fell silent. The kitchen clock echoed in Edgar's eardrums.

"How did you end up in a grade-four class, Edgar?" Ms. Lajoie asked.

Edgar twiddled the pen. He clicked it uncomfortably. *I liked it when I was in grade four*, he wrote finally.

He waited. Ms. Lajoie had a vein in her neck, like a pale

blue river beneath the milky white surface. Throb, throb.

"If we moved him to seven–eight," Ms. Lajoie said—then she turned to Edgar. "If we moved *you* to the grade seven-eight class, Edgar, you'd be in with Caroline, but with Jason, too, and maybe we don't want that. Any class you go into—"

I have the right class now, he wrote. *You are the best teacher for me.*

"But now that I know that you're actually eleven years old—" Ms. Lajoie said.

I love you, Edgar wrote.

"Edgar!" His mother took the pad away, as if she could cause Ms. Lajoie to unread the statement. "Sometimes he suffers from an excess of honesty," his mother said.

Ms. Lajoie looked at her fingernails: short, shaped, clean.

It was true: he loved Ms. Lajoie, just as he loved his old teacher, Ms. Nordstrom, too, even though he would never see her again. And he loved Caroline, he loved Victoria, and Benjamin. He loved the hillside in that light. . . .

Could she see all that in the way he was looking at her?

"I can let you stay for now," she said. "We'll figure out a course of reading. Maybe when you feel safer, you'll find your voice again."

ROAST

THE LATENESS OF THE AFTERNOON TURNED into evening, and Ms. Lajoie had not left, so Edgar's mother invited her for dinner. By that time Ceese had dropped by with pot roast that Jason's mother had cooked after talking some more with her son. Ceese said she was too embarrassed to bring it herself, she felt so awful for what Jason had done to Edgar. So Ceese stayed for dinner too, and Caroline came with an apple cobbler she had made all by herself, and she wanted Edgar to know she was personally going to beat up Jason unless he stopped being such a dork.

"It's a funny thing," Ms. Lajoie said at the table when extra chairs had been found (the cobbler was delicious with ice cream; it made Edgar's throat feel velvety), "but I had a cousin once in Calgary who barked like a dog for a time. We thought he was going to need special treatment.

Lasted all summer, I think, but he grew out of it. He's an accountant now."

"I had a cousin who used to sniff fence posts like a dog," Ceese said. They were all smiling now. It was not serious. The evening had come to feel like a party.

I wish I had a cousin, Edgar wrote.

"All the dogs in Dawson are your cousins!" Ceese said, and—maybe it was coincidence—in the distance several dogs started barking. The kitchen fell silent. Then Edgar's mother exploded in laughter the way that she could, and everyone else followed.

Ceese and Edgar's mother, Edgar's mother and Ceese. They barely looked at each other, but when they did, the coffeepot boiled, the window pane started a low, electric trembling.

Ms. Lajoie whispered close to Edgar—loud enough for everyone to hear, "You know, you could run a fair business in this town telling people what their dogs really think of them."

"Don't say that!" Edgar's mother blurted. "Edgar's too honest already! We'd be run out of town in hours!"

It was odd to hear everyone, to understand so well what they were all saying, and yet to stay silent. Or at least it was odd for Edgar to be allowed to simply sit and watch people talk about him.

Word spread. Maybe Ceese contacted his friends, but suddenly others began to show up because a party was happening. Some were from the party on the first night at Ceese and Caroline's, and some Edgar didn't recognize. He waited for Victoria to come through the door, for her to sit on the sofa with her arm around Ceese's big shoulders, because then it would be real—Edgar's mother could change, and just let Ceese go. But Victoria did not arrive, and instead his mother was drinking beer after beer, standing against the living room wall, with her socked foot on the sofa arm where Ceese's large hands naturally started to rub, and she did not even change her conversation.

That was how easy it was to steal him.

More people came; there was music. An angular miner named Jake started barking at Edgar. He said exactly, "Ruff-ruff. Ruff-ruff-ruff!" and then stared at Edgar, grinning stupidly, waiting for a reply. Ms. Lajoie excused herself, but not before she took Edgar aside and said, "You will be safe in my classroom. I don't want you to worry about a thing."

Ceese told Caroline it was time to leave, but then Edgar's mother touched his neck as she was heading into the kitchen for another drink, and he stayed on.

When did people start talking about the pictures? Edgar didn't know. But at some point someone was showing a picture he'd found on a street corner of a woman's purse, and wasn't the same purse right here—Stephanie's? And then someone else had a picture of Chief Isaac, and were these Stephanie's boots, too?

His mother was in the kitchen. She was getting another drink. Edgar waited for the explosion, but maybe she was feeling too good to know it must've been him. . . .

"Edgar," she said finally, when the picture of her empty sweater was in her hand and she could not avoid it. "What the hell are you up to?"

"Don't be too hard on the boy," Ceese said. His eyes seemed to be saying, *Let's all just skate past this trouble here, whatever it is.*

"I don't understand. Why did you take these pictures of my *boots*? My *lipstick*? And then scatter them around?"

He'd gone too far, too far. He had no way to say he was sorry.

"Let's just drop it," Ceese said softly. Everyone was around. They were all listening. The party was at a standstill.

"He already dropped it. He dropped pictures of my things all over town. *Why?* Edgar, *why?*"

She was looking like she really wanted an answer.

Edgar was roasting, roasting. He bit his lip.

Everything passes. Even this moment. When all the breath is frozen in the room.

"If I wasn't drunk . . . ," she said finally in a little voice, the thought trailing off into nothing.

The party did not end there. More people arrived carrying bottles, and cases of bottles. Then it *was* as if everything were forgotten. Edgar fell asleep in his bed listening to his mother singing sweetly in the living room, above the noise of the crowd, something about angels, angels in the harbor. The house smelled of bodies, of warmth, of cigarettes and other smoke, of adults opening themselves the way they could sometimes, unpeeling almost.

He drifted in and out of sleep. The bear was close, smell-able but out of earshot. Soon, when the bear was asleep, Edgar would get up and help his mother to her own bed. She did not always make it there herself. Edgar had watched Ceese accept her socked foot, had seen his face when she had touched his neck, when he was trying to get her past being furious and sad. He was a funny man, bighearted. He might not—probably would not—be able to keep himself from all the coming knots. If only the bear weren't breathing so loudly! But soon, soon Edgar would get up and release Ceese. That's what he would do, release Ceese from having to lead Edgar's mother to her own bedroom.

Maybe . . . maybe soon.

(He could hear his mother's voice, sometimes, and then he couldn't. And the bear stank like it would never, ever leave, so when . . . when would be the precise, exact time to move?)

Edgar was walking again along the ice, the ice and snow. The river played a longing song underfoot. He didn't have this camera. The hills would not be bathed in gold, but maybe the moon . . .

(He was only dreaming. The feeling would not be the same. What he had now was an echo of the very best moment of this afternoon. That was what a memory was, a ripple on water, longing for stillness. He had to be ready to appear beside his mother, at just . . .

. . . the right

. . . time.)

Still.

Still.

Benjamin farted. It wasn't the bear, not the bear at all . . . and the world was still, which meant . . . maybe it was too late.

Nighttime, soft steps. The darkness was filled with the smells of the dead party. Edgar was late, late, too late. He knew it in his own socked feet. As soon as his mother had lifted her toes to the sofa arm beside where Ceese had been sitting . . . as soon as she had touched his waiting neck . . . and Ceese had spoken up so that she wouldn't explode everything over Edgar's strange pictures . . .

(And they *were* strange. He could see that now. He could be a strange person sometimes. So could anyone. But how would anyone else know that the pictures were smells, smells on the roadside that told the news about Edgar's mother, who she really was? And yet the pictures had been found. Some part of the news was getting out.)

Quiet. Bottles on the bookshelves. Glasses on the floor, some tipped. Cigarette smoke hanging. Maybe . . . maybe she was passed out on the sofa.

(How many times had he come upon her passed out on a sofa?)

Just one more time. *Please.*

But the sleeper on the sofa was Caroline, tucked under a comfy blanket. Everyone else was gone.

Was that true?

Where was Ceese?

But it did not mean . . .

It did not mean Edgar should creep down the stairs to his mother's room. (He stood still, picturing himself placing one foot after the other, descending the carpeted steps.)

It did not mean he should stand in front of her closed door listening for their sounds, smelling what he would smell.

It did not mean—

Footfalls from his mother's room, coming up the stairs—heavy! A door shutting softly, care being taken.

The flush of the toilet. Edgar could almost feel how lightly the hand pressed on the handle. Then the door opening, those heavy feet returning down the stairs.

Voices. Whispers. If he stopped breathing, he could hear:

"I have to go."

"Do you?" Her drinking voice, so soft . . .

"Where's my—"

"Do you?"

"I don't think I—"

"Can't you?"

Large bodies on the bed.

"Stephanie, I—"

"Shhh."

"I really—"

"Oh, shhh!"

And then breathing. And the rest.

DARKNESS

THEY WERE HALFWAY DOWN THE HILL INTO town, the darkness swallowing them, before Benjamin asked where they were going.

"West Dawson," Edgar said, his breath clouding the way before him. The road was especially slippery. It had thawed somewhat in the highest sun of the day, and refrozen slickly now in the cold night. Edgar's boots were not leather, had no fur, did not embrace his calves warmly. The soles barely had treads; he felt like he was walking with a flimsy strip of rubber between him and the cold earth.

(The man in the story, the one who fell through the ice and froze before he could make a fire, had far warmer clothes than Edgar now wore. But Edgar wasn't going to fall through any ice.)

"Why are we going to West Dawson?" Benjamin wheezed. Back at the house he had been deeply asleep. Edgar had needed to shake him, to pinch his ears, before he woke up.

"That's where Victoria lives."

The hill was not so steep, or so long. Soon enough the road flattened out. The houses all were still, dark, either empty or simply bedrooms for sleeping bodies.

"I like Victoria," Benjamin panted. "Haven't seen her for a while."

"Then you know how to get to her house?" Edgar said. His boots squeaked on the frozen road. He felt sure that in a moment his body would warm up the way he had warmed on the walk that afternoon. Maybe he could catch another glimpse of something that would flash through him—the moonlight on the ice, the shadows cloaking the trees—and he would warm through to the roots of his hair. It was dark, but he had his camera with him, the strap around his shoulders. The camera bumped against him with the jolting of his steps.

He was shivering; his teeth felt chilled.

"West Dawson is across the river," Edgar said. Not abandoned at all.

"I haven't been across the river in a long time," Benjamin said. "Where's the car?"

"We're walking!" Just at that moment Edgar stubbed his toe on a chunk of ice and stumbled. The shock reminded him of how frigid he felt in his shoulders and arms.

They walked along the flat of the town. The moon looked cold too, wrapped in foil.

"Is it far across the river?" Edgar asked. "Can we see West Dawson?"

Across the river was black hills, purple sky. No lights whatsoever. But West Dawson had no electricity.

"Do you know Rupert?" Edgar asked. Victoria's dog.

"Rupert is just a puppy," Benjamin said. He was walking slowly. Had Edgar dragged him too far already that afternoon?

Well, Edgar couldn't stay in the borrowed house with Ceese and his mother. So he would have to get to West Dawson with Benjamin.

And he couldn't wake Caroline. There would've been too much to explain.

Why wasn't Edgar warming up? There was no wind. The air was still, but cold too, like something that did not want him walking through it.

In West Dawson there would be Victoria's fire, which Benjamin loved. Edgar could say hello to Rupert and ask him about the wolves.

The tips of the hairs on Benjamin's muzzle were frosted

white. Edgar felt his eyes tear up. When he blinked, they stayed shut for a moment, almost frozen.

"To get to Victoria's house," Benjamin said, "someone drives you in the car. It's warm till you open the door to go out."

"We have no car. We're going to walk."

They *were* walking. Through the quiet town, past the ghostly wooden buildings. Lola's bar, shut up and still. Someone else must have been on shift earlier tonight. Why not Edgar's mother? None of this would've happened. Ceese would not have stayed.

Past the big yellow building with the ballroom inside, where Edgar had heard Victoria sing her song, with Ceese on drums and Edgar's mother quietly fuming.

A few more blocks, then they crossed Front Street and climbed the rise to the edge of the river.

"Why don't you get a car and drive us there?" Benjamin panted.

"West Dawson is just on the other side. Isn't it?" Edgar said.

They had walked much farther that afternoon. But it was colder now. Edgar's face felt chilled into a squint. And the other side of the river, which didn't look all that far away, was in darkness—hills and trees, not a town, not anything that showed up.

"The car would get us there without freezing our paws," Benjamin said.

Down the side of the bank. The trail appeared immediately. The ice roadway was to the left, a detour. Why not just head straight across? The snow and ice were lumpy, but they would support Edgar's weight. "We'll save time," Edgar said.

He had not brought a leash. He had taken it for granted that Benjamin would accompany him, that the dog would want as much as Edgar did to get out of the house, to *do* something. But Benjamin stayed up on top of the bank, sniffing, while Edgar looked up at him from below.

"We'll warm up if we keep moving," Edgar said.

"We'll warm up if you get the car," Benjamin called down.

"I don't have a car. I can't drive. I'm just a kid. I've never done it!"

"Then let's go back inside and forget all this until Ceese drives us."

"But Ceese is with my mother now. He isn't with Victoria anymore!"

Benjamin looked away, upriver. Probably he couldn't really understand what humans did, the problems they made for themselves.

"It ruins everything!" Edgar called up to him. "My

mother won't keep him. She never does. But Victoria will explode, or she'll cry till she's sick. I don't know." He had seen his mother do these things and more, when men were concerned.

Benjamin sniffed, sniffed, as if he couldn't quite fathom it.

"It's what people do," Edgar said. "It feels like everything is coming apart."

"Why do we need to be there when it does?" Benjamin asked.

It was a fair question. Benjamin turned away.

"Victoria might stop my mother," Edgar said. "She could talk to Ceese and wake him up. She could—"

Benjamin disappeared behind the slope. Probably he was shambling back toward his warm blanket at the borrowed house where Ceese and Edgar's mother were doing what they were doing.

"If you don't come with me, I won't know where I'm going. I might fall through the ice!" Edgar said, although he didn't think he would. The open stretch was down a ways.

Silence. Then he thought he heard the huff of Benjamin's breath getting farther away.

Enough! Edgar didn't need Benjamin. The old dog would just slow him anyway. Edgar headed straight across.

It was face-smacking cold, but if he saw open stretches, the black water, he'd just walk around. It wasn't far, really. And Victoria's house had to be somewhere in the woods beyond.

He had to get to Victoria because she understood about the pictures and about him, and because of something he had heard in her voice when she had sung her song. She had her own black water, her own open stretches where the world ran so cold, it could swallow her up. One wrong step—it wouldn't take much. That was what her song had been about, beneath the surface. It was one thing for Edgar to fall in love with Ms. Lajoie and others. That was like breathing. It took no effort. But old people like Victoria, like Ceese and Edgar's mother—when they fell in love, it was like that man in the story falling through the ice and floundering around, telling himself what to do but not being able to save his fingers from the cold.

Edgar fell in love all the time. He had a sense of it. Ms. Nordstrom, Ms. Lajoie, Caroline, Victoria. The light on the hills this afternoon—just looking. That too was a sort of falling in love.

Edgar could fall and bend, he could be in love with all of it yet still make porridge in the morning. But old people—

The ice and snow were harder to navigate than Edgar

had expected. Sometimes his boots broke through and he had to adjust, find his balance. He didn't break through all the way to water—that seemed impossible, given the thickness of the ice chunks already thrown up by the shifting river—but through the crust into softer parts. The trail would've had better footing, but it led out of the way—back to the ice road, quite a distance upriver from where he was now. If he just kept straight—

He got closer and closer to the darkness of open water.

I must be tired, he thought. *I know the black is water, but I keep walking toward it anyway. As if—*

As if he couldn't make his mind believe there *could* be any open water at all on a cold, cold night like this.

Edgar fought against the bad footing. He slid, broke the crust, righted himself. It was quicker this way to get across.

"I am telling myself a story," he said, not very loudly, but it was a quiet night. This was Dawson. Maybe the whole town could have heard him if everyone hadn't been sleeping. (Or pretending to sleep.)

It was an odd feeling, almost fighting with himself, knowing and not knowing. Benjamin had stayed on the shore, had headed back to his warm blanket. Benajmin wasn't telling himself a story about searching for Victoria when in fact he was walking, stumbling, picking his way straight toward the blackness of open water, and why?

How else was Edgar going to understand the way his mother lived her life?

His mother would not think of Victoria, so Edgar had to. If that was a story, it was a good one, a true one.

True enough.

"Hey! Hey! Boy!" Benjamin called from somewhere behind him. Edgar turned. It was hard to see a black dog, even a big one, on a black night. "Come back here! Get away from the edge! Stupid humans!"

Edgar smiled. He wasn't even close to the edge, but it was nice to know that Benjamin hadn't really abandoned him.

"I'm all right. I'm going to go around," Edgar said calmly. He knew what he was doing. Didn't he?

"Get back here! Don't make me come get you!"

It was an interesting feeling, to be turning to look at the big black dog, and yet after a time not really moving his feet. *People spin in movies all the time*, Edgar thought. Now somehow, on the ice, without even moving, he was . . .

. . . moving.

"Stay where you are! I'll come get you!" Finally Edgar could see Benjamin. He was shambling like the bear, scrambling over the lumps of ice and snow as if there were something to hurry about.

"I'm not going to—"

But something *was* happening. The ice itself was moving, or at least the part Edgar was standing on. It spun slowly and shifted along beside other chunks of ice not moving at all. Edgar couldn't see the water—not close to him—but he was heading along anyway. Benjamin now was behind him slightly, still a distance off, adjusting—

"I didn't mean to!" Edgar called.

The ice and snow beneath his feet were as solid as ever. But now the river was pulling him along.

Not seriously. The chunk of ice Edgar stood upon was very large, and where was there to go? The stretch of black water didn't last long before Edgar's patch of ice bumped against another huge one in slow motion. Edgar took a step forward and three steps back, but kept his balance. His camera clunked against him. Chunks of ice on the edge of the sheet broke off and piled up on the other section, the one they had hit. Edgar could see all around him now many more broken blocks of ice pushed up by these sorts of collisions. The black stretch of water was fairly short. Most of this section of the river was frozen still. It was just an unexpected ride.

Lucky. Like the encounter with the bear.

He hadn't really meant to get anywhere near the edge. "It's all right!" he called. "Benjamin—I'm fine!" Edgar scanned the darkness, the edge of white against black, for his friend. He skipped back off the movable ice and stood once more on a solid patch. "I'm over here!" he called.

No movement. No return call.

"Benjamin! Benjamin!"

Edgar headed back along the line of last sighting. Benjamin had been gaining on him. He ought to be just about here.

Back, back. Picking his way. Edgar looked for tracks. Probably Chief Isaac, of the Tr'ondëk Hwëch'in, was a good tracker and would have been able to see exactly—

"Benjamin!"

Nothing. And then—movement, there, in the blackest part of the night. Benjamin was lying down but holding his head up, raising his paw. He must've been exhausted. After all the walking he'd done lately.

Edgar hurried toward him. "It's okay. We'll rest here and then—"

But Benjamin wasn't lying down. He was stuck. His head and shoulders were above the ice; his front paws were hanging on while the rest of him was splashing below.

Edgar felt sick all at once, curdled inside. His body went sour and weak at a stroke. *"Hold on! Benjamin!"* The first step he took was crazy. He'd guessed badly where the ice and snow below him might be, and he fell over hard, whacked his elbow and his chin. He lay there groaning, trying to get his body back.

"Don't sink! Don't die!" he called.

He was sick on the ice. The pot roast and cobbler dinner came out of him, his body knowing before he did, somehow, that this was all his fault. If he hadn't insisted on walking straight out—

"I'm coming!" Edgar called.

He groaned and rolled. His camera caught on the ice, and he threw it off him as if it were trying to pull him under. "Benjamin, Benjamin!"

Edgar regained his feet dizzily. He wasn't seeing well. He was the man in the story fumbling so badly.

But he wasn't far from Benjamin, whose head—calm, true, not panicking—still stuck out in the darkness.

"I'm coming!" Edgar squeaked, in hardly his voice at all—his jaws felt screwed shut. He stumbled again. *My fault! All of this!*

"Just leave me," Benjamin said. "You're not going to—"

What? Edgar was already there. He pitched forward onto the slushy ice (how could anything be thawing in this cold, cold?) and grabbed Benjamin behind the shoulders.

"You're not strong enough. Just—"

Edgar pulled. Benjamin slipped, nearly went under,

but his great paws scratched the edge of the ice, barely holding himself up.

"*Save yourself!*" Benjamin barked.

Edgar's mitted fingers plunged into the water and found Benjamin's collar. He pulled and pulled. He wasn't strong enough to lift a beast like Benjamin, but he could pull a bit. . . .

Edgar rolled back, still hanging on. He was small, but sometimes even a meager pull at the right time can shift the balance. Benjamin grasped stronger ice at last. He struggled free and stood for a moment, stunned and immobile, fully on the ice again, then shook himself and his freezing fur until his fur stood out, instantly stiffened in the cold air, and Edgar too was covered in a fine sheen of ice.

"I'm sorry! I'm so, so sorry!" Edgar said.

But there wasn't time to be sorry now. If they stood there any longer—

"This way!" Edgar said, and pulled on Benjamin's collar just to get him moving. Where? Around the black water. It wasn't far. Over the chunks and the blocks of semisolid crashed ice to the darkness where West Dawson must be. "Just run! Just run!"

They scrambled, slipped, got up. It wasn't far. It wasn't—

"Run! Run!" Edgar panted again. It felt like his hand was frozen to Benjamin's collar. If the dog went under again, Edgar didn't think he could let go. They would sink together. It would be better that way. (How awful that had been, to look back in the dark and see no Benjamin.)

"Just run! Run!"

They shambled together. It all became a blur, a slosh of ice chunks and snow and scrambling with a vague sense that the shore ought to be there. It should be—

It was! The ice road, there it was, this end of it running parallel to the shore.

They were running now to warm up, to drive their blood to parts of their bodies that the cold was ready to claim. Edgar's hand felt welded to Benjamin's collar. They ran together as if this were some sort of strange community competition. (Not a three-legged race. Edgar had been in one of those at school back in Toronto. But instead a boy-and-dog race.) They had to—

—make it along the ice road, and climb the hill that was the far bank—

"Where is it?" Edgar asked, gasping. He really wasn't a good runner.

Neither was Benjamin. They both trembled in the cold and dark up on the bank by the ice road.

"How do you get to West Dawson from here?" Edgar croaked.

You take a car. Benjamin didn't even have to say it. The thought barged through Edgar's mind. You take a car and continue climbing the hill along the road that circled into darkness somewhere beyond what Edgar could see.

PADDLEWHEEL

"SO WHERE EXACTLY IS VICTORIA'S HOUSE?" Edgar asked now. They were on the road halfway up the hill. "You must be able to smell it from here."

Edgar could see no houses. The road led upward through bush, snow, and rock. But on the right . . . was something. Another, smaller road.

"Is this the way?" Edgar asked.

Possibly Benjamin couldn't hear him. Possibly it was all Benjamin could do to keep his head down and follow the lead of Edgar's dangerously stiff right hand, his mitted fingers curled so tightly around the dog's collar. They started down the smaller road—why not? If they were lucky, it would lead to the houses of West Dawson, one of which had to be Victoria's.

"Is this the way? Do you remember this road?" Edgar asked.

Downhill now. Silent except for their ragged breathing. As long as they kept moving, Edgar thought, they would be all right.

Benjamin whispered, "Just call." His voice was as brittle as the air seemed to be.

"I don't have a phone," Edgar said. "I don't have a car. I'm human, but I don't have those things."

"Just call . . . out."

"But who is going to understand a word I say?" Edgar replied. "All I can do is—"

Bark. Bark like a dog.

"Hey! Hey!" Edgar called. "I'm here with Benjamin. He fell through the ice. We're freezing. Where's Victoria's house? Anybody?"

As echoey as sound seemed to be out on the frozen river, in the woods now, Edgar's voice felt swallowed, muffled.

"My name is Edgar!" he called more loudly. Was he barking, or speaking like a boy? He had no idea. "I'm here with Benjamin, the Benjamin you know. We need help, help!"

Nothing. This road was leading into woods, that was all. Nothing more.

"Let me know if you hear me, at least!" Edgar called.

On other nights they had heard plenty of dogs barking in the distance, and it had sounded like they were all the way across the river in West Dawson—packs of them. Were they all sleeping now? Why could no one hear him?

The road was leading them through a campground, apparently. There were signs and snowy flat sections where tents might go if it were summer.

"If we're going the wrong way . . . ," Edgar said.

They would die. Like the man in the story who could not make a fire.

"Victoria!" Edgar called. The cold air swallowed her name.

And the road ended . . . nowhere: trees, snow, silence. As Edgar glanced desperately in all directions, Benjamin trembled, his head sagging.

"I can smell a fire," Benjamin whispered at last.

"Where?"

Benjamin lurched forward onto a path Edgar could not even see. Edgar had to follow, frozen by the hand to the big dog's collar.

"Down here. Here," Benjamin muttered.

Down here was . . . the river again. The ice-packed shore. Edgar could see no fire anywhere. Just darkness.

"There are no houses," Edgar said. "I didn't see any smoke or—"

But the dog pulled him along. How had Edgar ever summoned the strength to hoist Benjamin out of the river? Edgar felt as light as driftwood now, tethered to the solid neck of a determined beast.

"There is a fire," Benjamin breathed. "Can't you smell it?"

Edgar couldn't smell anything. Maybe his senses were shutting down. The scene around him felt jumbled, the black trees and the white river ice, his footsteps louder than a train's wheels, his face a frozen mask.

They were following the river, on something of a footpath. Were the houses along here? There, back in the bush, was a structure, but it looked desolate, empty. Could this be West Dawson?

Abandoned.

That's what the map had said.

"It's here. It's . . ."

But it wasn't a fire. Not a real one. On the shore ice lay the remnants of a fire: charred sticks and old, blackened river stones. Cold.

"Can't you smell them?" Benjamin said.

"Who?"

Faintly Edgar could just get a sense of several . . . kids who had been here sometime, maybe days ago.

But there was no smoke, no heat, no . . . hope. Benjamin shuddered, still standing, beside Edgar. If only Edgar could release his hand from Benjamin's collar!

His eye caught something rising from the darkness of the woods. It looked like . . . immense dinosaur bones, a skeleton of some sort—

"What's that?" he exclaimed.

Benjamin's head was down. He was sniffing the dead ashes still.

Edgar took a step back, and the dog lurched with him. "Benjamin!"

The dog's head had become so heavy. His coat had hardened into spiky black frozen fur. Edgar tried to brush off some of the ice with his free hand.

"It's the Paddlewheel Graveyard," Benjamin said. "For the old riverboats." He slumped beside the cold remains of the fire that would have saved them, maybe, if it still had been going. Edgar knelt with him.

Caroline had told him about this place. The remaining structures looked like the bones of old beasts. There was smashed planking and cracked hulls, places where the ice of many winters must have crushed lengths of decking. And there—a huge paddle wheel rising out of the snow. And others behind it.

"I'm sorry," Edgar said, patting the big dog's frozen head. Why hadn't he woken Caroline? She would've known where to go, what to bring. "If I had matches," Edgar said, "there's plenty of wood we could burn."

"There are worse places," Benjamin said.

To die, he meant.

Both of them were going to die—Benjamin because he was wet and frozen and old and exhausted, and Edgar because he was small and cold and couldn't release his hand from Benjamin's collar.

Probably everybody in the Yukon carries matches, Edgar thought. It would only be sensible. And a knife. He had set out to cross the broken ice of the Yukon River without matches or a knife, just as stupidly as the man in the story had set out on his long journey in the woods all alone except for his dog.

Edgar had been alone too. Why?

It was easy to think more clearly now that there was nothing he could do. This was surely much worse than lying in bed in the borrowed house listening to his mother and Ceese. Benjamin had been asleep already; it would not have ruined either of their lives for Edgar to know what mothers and others got up to.

No. Edgar had dragged them both out here. He had acted worse—even more stupidly wild—than his mother.

Benjamin became very still, and Edgar gazed at the bones of the paddle wheels. They looked like they'd been thrown up onto the beach by some careless giant who didn't want to play with them anymore.

"I'm sorry, Benjamin," Edgar whispered, stroking the dog's huge head with his free hand. He stared at the collar bound to his mitten, and slowly, slowly realized the dog's collar could come off. There was the buckle, knobby under a sheen of ice. He could pull off his left mitt with his teeth and use his still-moving fingers to unbuckle the collar. Just because Benjamin was dying . . .

But there was peace here. It would be cold, and it would be quiet. Surely he wouldn't feel the pain of it much longer.

"Benjamin," Edgar said. "Are you dying?" Edgar could still feel Benjamin's breath in some part of his bone-chilled hand.

"Looks like," Benjamin whispered, then stayed quiet. Had Benjamin slipped into sleep? Would this be the last he would hear—

But the dog roused himself. "Never died before," he said.

"Did you mean to bring us here?" Edgar asked.

How cold the silence. Edgar got a sense of it suddenly—how cold and long it would be, to not have Benjamin's voice for company.

But—not yet. "We should have taken a car," Benjamin groaned.

"Are you in pain?" Edgar said. "I'm sorry! I'm sorry for all of this. I didn't know this would be so close."

He meant the end of everything.

But Benjamin maybe thought something different. "It is close," he breathed. "In the car."

Was it? Were they just a short walk from Victoria's house, after all? The man in the story was miles from anyone when he froze. There really was no hope for him. But people did live somewhere on this side of the river. Maybe close to the Paddlewheel Graveyard? Maybe Edgar could free the collar himself and go get help in time for Benjamin, after all? He was a big strong dog. Maybe he wouldn't die so easily.

Maybe—maybe Edgar needed to try.

"Benjamin," Edgar said. "Do you want me to try to get help? Or—stay here with you?" He didn't say "while you die."

It might be a horrible thing to die alone.

"Benjamin?"

"Why don't you," Benjamin said, "get the car?"

Edgar shoved his left hand between his knees and pulled until his mitt came off. His right, even in a mitt, was smarting fiercely, curled around Benjamin's icy collar. His left felt freshly alive, although it would be just a matter of minutes, Edgar felt—maybe seconds—before it too started to hurt shockingly.

Benjamin's collar was made of thick, stiff leather, now frozen solid. Edgar gripped the buckle as tightly as he could. Ceese, with his huge hands, would have worked the strap free in a moment, Edgar thought. Roger, too. But Edgar's fingers slipped off feebly. He made a fist and hit the buckle three, four times. Bits of ice came off, but the buckle strap wouldn't budge. Finally he bit at it, but that was pitiful. Surely his mouth would freeze to the buckle.

He was weak, weak, all the way through. "When was the last time you had your collar off?" he moaned.

Benjamin shifted onto his side. "Never," he snorted.

"Well, you have to get up!" Edgar snapped.

Benjamin was old. Maybe he couldn't move anymore.

But maybe he could. "Come on! Come on!" Edgar said. He shoved his left hand back into his mitt. The collar wasn't budging, he couldn't free himself. So Benjamin would have to rise again and come with him.

"I think the car is this way!" Edgar said suddenly.

"Bring it here," Benjamin muttered. "Make it warm."

"We can't. There's no road. We have to walk to it," Edgar said.

"You go."

"I can't! I can't!" Edgar pulled hard but only slightly lifted the giant dog's neck and head.

Benjamin groaned, then farted.

"You're not dead yet!" Edgar said. "And neither am I!"

"You go. Just let me—"

"If you can fart, you can stand up!" Edgar said. For a moment he felt hot through much of his body. From his knees he jerked upward with both hands.

Benjamin groaned, whirled, and bit harmlessly at Edgar's jacketed arm. Edgar shifted his balance and stood, dragging Benjamin halfway up.

"Let's go back and get the car!" Edgar said.

Up, up, unsteadily Benjamin stood. He looked sadly at the bones of the paddle wheels, as if he wanted to just stay here with them.

"You can fart all you want in the car," Edgar said.

They started back along the shore. It was still dark, but there was a path to follow. It would return them to the road, and the road would lead to West Dawson. To people. To heat.

It had to.

"Did you call someone . . . ," Benjamin huffed, "to bring the car?"

"I did. I did!" Edgar felt almost giddy with the lie. "They're waiting right now. Just along here."

Benjamin did not pick up the pace, but he did not slow either. Edgar thought: *We can't be dead if we're moving.*

"I wish you had called earlier," Benjamin said. He

kept his head low. Edgar pulled but not too hard.

"I wish I'd just stayed in bed!" Edgar said.

"Yes, yes, yes," Benjamin puffed.

They were moving, they were moving. It was farther than Edgar remembered, but here was the trail at last, in from the shore. And here . . . was where it joined the campsite road.

Where no one was camping.

"We can sleep in the car," Edgar said. The more he talked about the car, the more it seemed there *would* be a vehicle of some sort, waiting somewhere. Ceese's truck maybe. Edgar's mother might have recognized by now that Edgar was gone. She would have sent Ceese out, and he would track them to this very spot. He would have matches, and a knife, and warm blankets. And his truck would be warm. Edgar remembered how Ceese had stopped on the highway to pick up Edgar and his mother walking in from the airport. He had helped Edgar's mother first. A gentleman. Now if Edgar and Benjamin just kept walking . . .

But Benjamin was shaking, wheezing.

"Don't say a thing," Benjamin whispered, "to the wolf."

Edgar looked around quickly. "What wolf?"

"Don't even let him know . . . you know he's here."

Dark trees, gray snow, shadows everywhere. No wolves

that Edgar could see. Benjamin picked up his pace.

Edgar couldn't see anything else moving. There was no car; maybe there was no wolf, either.

The campsite road, which was just a trail really, turned uphill. They were heading back toward the main road.

"We will be out of your way soon!" Benjamin called out to something in the shadows.

"You are not, not, not in my way," said the wolf. Edgar couldn't see him yet, but his voice was tall somehow, as tough as an old tree.

"We're just out walking. We'll be home soon," Benjamin called back.

"Neither of you looks well," said the wolf.

(Edgar thought he could see him now, out of the corner of his eye, a large glimmer of gray slipping along, a threatening shadow.)

"Oh, we are fine," Benjamin said, in a big voice that sounded hollow.

"But you are stepping, stepping, stepping . . . lamely," said the wolf.

Benjamin hurried, then stumbled. Edgar had to pull hard just to keep them both upright.

"Why don't you rest?" said the wolf. "Lie down. Let the boy go home. You and I can chat while you gather your strength."

"I'm stuck to his collar!" Edgar blurted. "I can't let go! And if he stops now, he won't get up again!"

Benjamin butted Edgar's thigh.

"He's not the smartest boy in the world, is he?" said the wolf.

"I have a knife!" Edgar called back. "I'll cut you open if you come for us!"

They were so close to the main road. If only—

"No need for knives, knives, knives," said the wolf. "Just leave your friend with me. I wouldn't hurt a little boy walking home."

They'd made it! Edgar and Benjamin broke through the tree cover of the campsite trail and stood in the openness of the main road. Edgar was surprised to see how deserted it was. He'd almost convinced himself that Ceese would be there with his truck, carrying a rifle perhaps.

Caroline had a rifle, Edgar remembered now. She had mentioned it. And she had told him about the Paddlewheel Graveyard, and she certainly knew where Victoria lived. If she had come with him tonight—

The road to West Dawson angled upward still, and curved, disappearing into darkness. Behind them was the river, the broken ice. They couldn't chance another crossing.

But the wolf was sitting above them in the middle of the lane that headed to wherever Victoria's house might be.

"I don't see your knife," the wolf said.

He had gray, thick fur, and looked even bigger than Benjamin, and a lot stronger, as if he could bound over and knock them both down before Edgar could even draw out an imaginary knife anyway.

"We're on the road!" Edgar said. "I could call now, and a hundred dogs would come to our rescue!"

The wolf did not look away. It was as if the ground rumbled when he talked. "They are safe in their little huts on a cold night. Not many dogs, dogs, dogs come out here, no matter who is calling."

They could not run. Edgar felt it was beyond him. He and Benjamin stayed staring at the wolf while the ice of the river, somewhere behind them and down the road, pushed and groaned.

"Where's the car?" Benjamin whispered.

"It's coming," Edgar whispered back. "Maybe. But maybe not soon."

Benjamin snorted. He seemed to inflate himself. "You know the way to Rupert's house," he called to the wolf.

"Rupert!" the wolf said. "Rupert, Rupert, Rupert—the puppy dog?"

"You bring us to Rupert's house," Benjamin said, "and I will lie down for you and offer my neck. Wherever you like. Your favorite feasting place."

The wolf didn't move. He seemed perfectly relaxed, yet coiled, too, somehow, as if he might snap them both without a thought.

"I am very fond of Rupert." The wolf licked his lips. Then he brought his paw to his muzzle, as if cleaning something, and finally returned to his sentinel pose.

It was cold, cold on Edgar's face now. But the danger seemed to warm other parts of his body. Maybe Benjamin too was thawing a bit in reaction to the wolf.

They waited, waited. Finally Benjamin said, "Make up your mind now, or this will be a hard fight, and you have to kill both of us. I might bite your face off before you get to my throat. That would not be a bad way for me to go."

The wolf licked his paws, as if he hadn't heard.

Suddenly Benjamin shouted out, *"All you friends, we need you now, I'm here with the boy Edgar! Wolf! Wolf!"*

His voice filled the darkness, echoed off the hills and across the river and back. But the silence that returned was even deeper than before.

"Dogs, dogs, dogs," the wolf said. "They really don't want to get their paws cold."

Benjamin tilted his head suddenly. Edgar wasn't sure what he heard, or smelled, or saw. But something else was not right.

More slick gray movement in the shadows. Edgar

glimpsed something, then another thing. He smelled a number of other bodies.

Other wolves.

"My offer is this," Benjamin called again. "See us to Rupert's house. Keep the boy safe. I will meet you when and where you like, be your feast. I won't turn a tooth against you. If you make us fight, with all your clan, the boy will die and you will all be hunted and shot cold before two days are done. You know this to be true!"

The wolf looked away, his ears flattened, before returning his gaze again as if he hadn't heard, didn't care, was just sitting out on a barely-used road in the middle of the night enjoying the fresh frigid air.

Benjamin snorted suddenly, and said to Edgar, "Walk!" Then the two of them were in motion, climbing the hill toward where the wolf remained on guard.

Closer, closer.

"Do not run, do not flinch, make no sudden movement," Benjamin whispered to Edgar.

Closer.

When Edgar could see the wolf's flaring nostrils, he felt his throat tighten but did not stop.

"You know it's best," Benjamin muttered to the wolf, who moved, finally, just before the dog and boy would have run into him.

"There's a shortcut," the wolf huffed, and then he was a glint of gray disappearing into the bush.

"Call off the others if you want this to work!" Benjamin said.

"Others, others, others," the wolf breathed back, a voice already almost lost in the shadows. "They'll do what they like, now, won't they?"

It couldn't be far to Victoria's house, it couldn't be. And Benjamin, half-frozen as he was, must have known what he was doing. Edgar had to trust, trust. He certainly couldn't see very far. The forest floor was white and frozen, but the trees in the shadows brought an extra gloom. He and Benjamin might as well have been in outer space, that's how cold and dark it felt.

Edgar kept his eyes down, looking for the next footfall. Where was the wolf? Where were the other wolves?

"Are they gone?" Edgar whispered.

"Don't be so hopeful," Benjamin grumbled.

"But I don't—"

The icy path snaked uphill between the trees. There wasn't much room for Edgar to walk beside Benjamin, but he had to because his hand was still caught on the dog's collar. Was his hand frozen now? Would he need to have it cut off even if he did survive this night?

"Maybe when we get to Victoria's house, she will have a gun," Edgar whispered. Was Benjamin really going to surrender to the wolf once they got there? Surely Benjamin had only said so to fool the wolf. It was too much—for him to survive the river only to surrender because of Edgar.

"Shhh!" Benjamin said. "Don't think!"

"But she might. She might have a gun that can save us!"

The wolf growled then, hidden in shadows but very close by.

"Shhh!" Benjamin said again.

They were moving, they were moving, but were they really alive? Or awake? A bad dream might be every bit as crazy as this. Edgar shook his head, blinked, waited for the darkness to recede and for Benjamin to be lying on his mat on the floor back in their warm, warm borrowed house.

Step, step.

Was this even the right path to Victoria's house? Maybe the wolf was leading them both deeper and deeper into the woods.

"Benjamin—how do we know—"

Benjamin was keeping his head down. He was sniffing, sniffing as he went along.

What could Edgar smell? Nothing. Maybe he wasn't a dog-boy anymore. Surely the wolves would have smelled a thousand times stronger and meaner than Brottinger, for example. Surely the stench of them would have boiled Edgar's blood by now. Maybe he was too cold.

He wasn't going to make it to Victoria's house. He was going to die along the way, and Benjamin would be eaten by the wolves all for nothing.

Edgar tried to hurry. It was a comfort, at least, to be attached to as noble a friend as Benjamin, who had risked everything, time and again, to save him.

He would not be saved.

But Edgar hurried anyway, his body courageous for him. His body knew there wasn't much time left. Ceese would not be waiting with the truck, and Victoria would not have her rifle ready, and the dogs of West Dawson were strangely silent. Everything in the world now was step after step after step.

Why couldn't he even smell the wolves? He and Benjamin were surrounded. They must have been. He could feel their hunger. Or maybe that was what he was smelling now, above everything else, the terrible ache of how much the wolves wanted to tear his flesh and swallow him down in bloody chunks even while he would still be screaming.

"Benjamin . . . Benjamin, I'm afraid," Edgar said.

The dog was sniffing and walking. The ground was strangely far away.

"I . . . don't want them to get me!" Edgar said.

"Of course you don't!" Benjamin muttered.

"But why—why are things this way?"

"What way? We are close to Victoria's. It's the quickest way we could've come."

Were they? Really? Close? It seemed, vaguely, as if there were dogs barking after all. Had they been barking all along? Something rectangular stood out in the distance, man-made. Not a house. A . . . pen. Fenced-in. A half dozen dogs were barking, barking. They were close, but they sounded like they were on the other side of the hills or something. Benjamin was headed straight for them. Edgar had to follow, even if his feet felt separated from the ground.

Where were the wolves?

The dogs in the pen were going crazy. It was a strange and nearly silent dream. Edgar thought maybe one of them was Rupert, but they were just barking, not saying anything intelligible at all. Then—he saw the house, over there, in the shadows. A light flashed on. Who was that at the door? Victoria?

Did she have her rifle?

Benjamin had promised that he would go with the wolf after seeing Edgar to safety, but Edgar's hand was frozen to the dog's hardened collar, so Edgar couldn't let him go. No bargain could be honored. It was as simple as that.

Victoria stood at the door. A flash of her hair. Would the wolves bite off Edgar's hand, just to make Benjamin pay as he had promised?

Edgar wanted to say, "Where's your rifle?"

He wanted to say, "Get your gun!"

And, "Wolves!"

But he was falling, falling. It was so sad to be so close. He couldn't help it. He didn't know where the ground was anymore . . . and then he was on it. Benjamin was down too. Together they would be too heavy for Victoria to move inside, into the warmth.

Edgar thought, *This is a strange last thought to have.*

He thought, *If Ceese were here, he could lift both of us to safety.*

And, *I know where Ceese is.*

That is the trouble.

And, *I'm sorry, sorry, Benjamin, for what the wolves are about to do.*

VICTORIA

IT WAS WARM INSIDE. VICTORIA HURRIED
Edgar over to the wood stove and started to pull off his
hat and jacket.

"Get your gun," Edgar said, because Benjamin didn't
seem to be inside with them.

"Shh! You're safe now!" Victoria said. "Oh, honey, look
at you! What are you doing here? How did you—"

"But Benjamin!" Edgar tried to turn, to point to the
door, to the wolves outside.

"I need to take these cold clothes off you," Victoria
said. She was both kind and hard in the eyes, and she
wasn't listening, she didn't understand.

"Benjamin made a deal, but he only said it to—"

She was having a hard time getting his right arm out
of his frozen jacket. "Can you let go?" she said. "Can you
open your fingers at all?"

He couldn't. She would know that if she looked. But instead—

"Whose collar is this?" she asked.

"I told you—Benjamin's!"

"Benjamin's? Where is he? I didn't see him."

They were talking, just like humans. She could understand his words.

Or did she speak dog now?

"Am I barking right now?" Edgar asked.

The stove was warm. It was lovely. He felt like he couldn't stay awake another moment. But he could clearly see Victoria fighting with the collar in his hand, as tough and stiff as it was, how it wouldn't go through the cuff of his jacket sleeve.

"Barking? What do you mean?" Victoria said. "This whole thing is crazy! What are you doing here, out so late and on your own? How did you get here? Is your mother with you?"

She worked it, got the collar to bend and pass through the sleeve after all. It took him the longest time to realize the collar was broken, maybe even bitten through. Who had done that? Benjamin?

"Please go look outside! Benjamin was with me. And there were wolves and—"

The collar dropped to the floor when he shook his hand.

Had he chewed through it himself? His mouth was oddly . . . stiffly sore, cut even, on one corner. A little bit of blood. But how could he have chewed through such a stiff collar? He had tried to bite it off, he remembered. But it had been too cold. The buckle had been frozen stiff. He'd been too weak.

"I'm not going to leave you right now," Victoria said. If the wolf's voice was rough, a tall tree, then Victoria's was a concrete pillar at the moment. "I have to warm you, but we need to do it safely. All right?"

Edgar nodded.

"You got your hand wet, did you? I'm just going to leave it in your mitt for now and concentrate on your core. I don't want you going into shock. Did you do something stupid in the river?"

She was wrapping him with blankets, warming his middle.

Edgar started to get up, to go call Benjamin, but she pulled him back.

"Stay by the stove. We do your core first. We'll see how that goes. I'm going to let the health center deal with your hand later. You're going to need to stay awake so that I know I still have you. All right? What's your mother's number?"

Her face was fierce. Edgar could not look away.

"Your cheeks are not too bad. Your ears and nose are

all right. I'm guessing your feet are pretty cold, though. How did you get your hand wet?"

Why couldn't he talk like a dog now, so that she couldn't understand him, instead of bombarding him with questions that were only going to lead to trouble?

"Did you really just cross the river in the middle of the night? Edgar, you need to tell me. What we do in the next few minutes is crucial. Do you understand?"

Edgar nodded.

Victoria tugged off his boots and then his socks, and rolled on some woolen ones she took from her own feet. Then she found another pair to pull over his hands, even his right, which still was curled coldly inside his mitt.

"Don't try to rub your toes. We won't put them in warm water just yet. We'll just let you stabilize while I call for help. Edgar—" She was kneeling before him at eye level. "What's your mother's number?"

"She doesn't have a phone," he said.

"Then I'm going to call Ceese."

Edgar shook his head. Her eyes narrowed.

"Why shouldn't I call Ceese?" Victoria said. And then, *"Why are you here, Edgar?"*

She was breathing as if she'd been running.

Her phone was out already. She moved away from Edgar. The blankets were warm. He was able, at last, to look around. It was a cozy cabin, softly lit, with gas lamps. It was all one big room, with the black stove in the middle, a small kitchen—well, everything was small—the sofa, many books in shelves. A ladder leading somewhere. It hurt to move his neck. Was he frozen everywhere?

He turned anyway. The ladder led to another room, like an attic, with a bed. Where Victoria had been sleeping, probably, before—

"Yes, hi, it's me," Victoria said into the phone. "I have Edgar, here. . . . Yes, Edgar. He came out of the bush half-frozen. He's okay for now, but I'm going to need to get him to the health center." Her back was turned. Her free hand was in her hair. "He didn't want me to call you."

Edgar could hear Ceese's big voice through the phone from across the tiny room. "What's he doing with *you*?"

And then, unmissable—Edgar's mother's sleepy voice. "Ceese, who's that?"

"Have you got somebody there?" Victoria snapped.

Then from the phone, Edgar's mother's voice again: "Has something happened to Edgar?"

"Who the hell is that?" Victoria said.

Ceese said, "Victoria, listen—uh—" Then he didn't say anything.

Victoria threw her phone, hard, onto the sofa.

It was happening, it was happening. How had Edgar thought this was going to play out?

"I'm sorry!" he said.

"What the hell are you doing here?" Victoria shoved both hands to her head. She paced. There wasn't very far to go in the cabin. "Is your mother . . . *Are she and Ceese* . . . ?" When Edgar nodded, Victoria said, "So you crossed the bloody river! You half froze yourself—"

His hands and his feet were hurting, burning, his right hand now especially. Why hadn't he just stayed in bed? What had he thought was going to happen?

"I'm sorry," he said.

For everything. Everything he was doing.

"How did you even know to come here? You've never been here! For Christ's sake!"

Edgar began to cry then. It flooded out of him. It *was* all his fault, all of it! Now Benjamin was gone, and his mother would hate him, and Ceese, and Caroline, and Victoria. He sobbed, but he couldn't wipe his eyes. His hand was an aching, numb, senseless thing. He should've just stayed with Benjamin at the Paddlewheel Graveyard.

Is that where he'd bitten through Benjamin's collar? He felt again the cut corner of his mouth. Then all that with the wolves—

"Please, stop crying," Victoria said, with some gentleness. "You just blindsided me in the middle of the night. I really can't believe you're here. Yet you are. Don't go into shock on me, all right? I'll get you some warm water. Just sip it. Let's take things one step at a time." She took a big kettle off the stove and poured steaming water into a mug, then poured cold water in as well. She held the mug for him. "Slowly, okay?"

She let him have a little bit, a little bit.

"Now you start to tell me—why are you here?"

Edgar had some more of the warm water. "I don't know," he said.

She smiled strangely. He had a sense it was like ice breaking somewhere deep.

"You're just a little angel of chaos," she said.

The heat was hitting him now. He felt his head nodding, just like that, as if he couldn't hold anything back anymore. Did he really have to stay awake?

"Ceese was very nice to me and my mother," he said. "That was when I knew there would be trouble."

He woke with a start, Victoria shaking him. It hadn't been much of a sleep, a minute at most.

"Are you cold still? I should've taken your temperature as soon as you got in. Let's do it now, all right?" She pushed a thermometer into his mouth. He held it under his tongue.

"I'm going to keep you drinking warm water," she said. "How are your hands? I bet they're really starting to hurt."

They were numb still. He touched his right hand with his left, and the right, especially, felt like a piece of chicken in a frozen package.

She drew the thermometer from his mouth and put on glasses to read it.

"All right. All right," she said. "You're still cool." She pulled a woolen hat over his head and ears. "I'm sorry I yelled before. Ceese is my boyfriend. I know you know that."

Edgar nodded. She held out more of the warm water for him.

"And you saw them, is that what happened? You saw Ceese and your mother together?"

Nod again.

"And they weren't playing Parcheesi, I'm guessing."

She stepped to a cupboard and pulled out a pale red hot water bottle, filled it from the kettle, then wrapped it in a towel. She filled the kettle again and put it back on the stove, then fixed the hot water bottle underneath the blanket already wrapped around him. "I need to get you to the health center, but the heater in my truck is shot. I'll call Ceese back if I have to, but Desmond lives nearby. I can always borrow his truck. But Des doesn't have a phone, and I don't want to leave you just yet. You seem to be shivering less than when you came in. You tell me if something changes, all right? In a bit I'll run and get Des's truck."

The water bottle felt beautifully warm. He pressed it to his side and moved it around his chest.

Her phone whistled. She picked it up angrily and stared at the little screen.

"I ought to shoot you," she said into the phone.

Ceese's voice sounded tinny. "I'm sorry, I'm sorry, I'm sorry!"

She turned her back on Edgar and simply stood in the middle of the room flexing and unflexing the fingers of her free hand.

"How's the boy?" Edgar could hear Ceese finally ask.

"If you're asking if you should drive here in your heated truck and pick us up so we can go to the health center, then yes, somebody should, but not you."

Silence, flex, flex.

"But he's okay, though? Is it frostbite?"

"You should send somebody else, in your truck, with the heater blasting. And whoever it is should get here five minutes ago. Don't bring your lover!"

She threw the phone down again onto the sofa.

"How does this happen?" she said to Edgar. "Life is chugging along, you're with a great guy, and then the dogs start barking in the middle of the night and suddenly everything is garbage?"

"I'm sorry," Edgar said.

"I don't believe you are. You are something else entirely. You're—something else." She shook her head, but she didn't really seem to be angry at him.

"I didn't want to make you sad," he said. "I crossed the river, but Benjamin fell in, so I had to pull him out."

"How did you even know where I live!" Victoria exclaimed.

"The wolf showed me. Benjamin made a deal with him. Otherwise we would have stayed at the Paddlewheel Graveyard, freezing."

"The *wolf* showed you? *What?*"

"After the Paddlewheel Graveyard. Benjamin thought he smelled a fire. But it was all cold. I might have dreamed some of it."

Victoria reached for her parka off the wall by the door, then started pulling on her boots. "I think you're hallucinating. But you are here, and we can't wait. I've got to get Des's truck. I'll be back in minutes. Understand?"

He did not understand. "What about Benjamin? You've got to look for him! And bring your gun. The wolf was going to eat him!"

She left without taking anything. Did she even have a

gun? She had told Ceese she was going to shoot him.

Sometimes people say things they don't really mean.

Minutes passed. Edgar wondered if he was going to fall asleep again but he felt wide awake now. He wondered who would be driving Ceese's truck. But clearly Victoria didn't believe Ceese was going to send anybody. That was why she'd gone herself. Suddenly dogs were barking, and the cabin was filled with light from outside. A vehicle pulled up. Was she back already?

No, it was Ceese's truck. Edgar's mother burst through the door, half-dressed, her coat falling off her. "Oh, my baby, my baby!" she called. She flew at Edgar, crushed him in her arms, began at once to rub his socked hands. Victoria was back again shortly after.

"Don't do that! Don't rub—you'll damage the flesh!"

"Oh, my baby. Oh, my baby!" his mother moaned, and kept rubbing.

"I'm warming him slowly!" Victoria said. She pulled at Edgar's mother's arms. For a moment Edgar was sure they were going to start wrestling right there, rip his arm off between them.

"You're freezing, you're freezing. Oh, look at you!" his mother wailed.

Ceese was standing behind. "Stephanie," he said, "Victoria's right. You can't rub at frostbite—"

And Caroline was there too, in her parka, her face lined with sleep and worry.

Edgar's mother held Edgar's face between her hands. "Why are you even here?" She was crying the way he had known she would.

For a time everyone stayed quiet, except for Edgar's mother's moans.

"I'm going to take his temperature again. He's been hallucinating," Victoria said finally. Edgar's mother backed off just far enough to allow Victoria to insert the thermometer into his mouth. Edgar sucked on it while everyone watched. He remembered being watched like that when he was very small—his mother measuring his face with the full probe of her eyes.

Finally Victoria pulled out the thermometer. "What's his temperature?" Edgar's mother exclaimed.

"He's warming up," Victoria said coolly. She put the thermometer away.

"Warming up to *what*? What was he before?"

"He was 96.1 not too long ago. He's 97.3 now. Not too bad. But I need to warm his core before his extremities so that he doesn't go into shock. If that's all right with you." Victoria's glare was quiet murder.

"We need to get him to the hospital!" Edgar's mother said.

Victoria turned to Ceese. "I told you not to come. Not to bring *her*. And why did you bring Caroline?"

"Let's not make this about anything else," Edgar's mother said quickly. "Let's just look after Edgar. Thank you for taking him in. I really appreciate it."

"Yeah, well," Victoria said, "that's what we're all about here in the north. Taking care of one another."

Ceese didn't seem to know where to look. He straightened to his full height, however, and said, "We shouldn't wait too long. The Highways Department guys were right behind me. Must be a warm front moving in. They're getting set to close down the ice bridge. They might not even wait for first light."

Victoria's eyes widened. "I thought we had another week at least!"

"The ice is already on the move. Edgar, you were lucky to get across," Ceese said.

"Well, I'm not ready!" Victoria said to Ceese. "I was going to come stay at your place. Now you've gone and screwed that up, haven't you?"

Ceese looked nervously at Caroline. Then Victoria hit him in the chest with both palms, sending him back a step. "What the hell were you thinking? Huh? Huh? How are you supposed to keep up with your new thing while I was staying at your place? *Huh?*"

"Victoria—"

Edgar's mother moved between them. "Please! Let's focus. Focus! We need to get Edgar across the river now!"

"What new thing?" Caroline said. "Dad?"

Ceese said, "We'll talk about it later—"

Caroline glared. "Dad! Do you mean you and Edgar's mom—"

"I can't believe you brought your lover *and* your daughter!" Victoria said, shaking her head in disbelief.

"Well, you *could've* called an ambulance," Ceese snapped back.

Victoria's jaw dropped open. Even Edgar's mother turned on him. "Don't say stupid things! Let's just get in the truck. Hurry!" She reached for Edgar's coat, which was on the floor, and started trying to fit his arms back into the sleeves.

"I'm just saying—there *is* an ambulance," Ceese muttered.

"Yes!" Victoria cried. "Because why would I expect that my boyfriend would be able to drop everything and get here without some terrible inconvenience?" She turned to Edgar's mother. "Don't force him!"

Edgar's mother seemed confused for a moment. She knelt down to deal with Edgar's boots, which did not seem to want to fit back on his feet.

Victoria stood over her. "You know what? You know what? You and Ceese just take my truck, all right? Drive fast, there's no heater. Edgar and I will meet you in Emerg. I don't think we should travel together. Under the circumstances. Do you understand?"

Edgar's mother stood. The two women were now almost nose to nose. "I am not leaving my boy here!"

"Well, you sure as hell don't know what you're doing with hypothermia, and Edgar, for whatever reason, walked all the way here on his own. Ceese—" She did not turn away from Edgar's mother. "If we have to travel together right now, nobody might make it alive! You know what I'm saying, Ceese."

She was holding out the keys, holding them out.

"Hang on a minute! *You* don't have to come to the hospital!" Edgar's mother said to Victoria. "We're done here!"

Gently Ceese went to Edgar's mother. "It's fine, it's fine," he murmured. "Stephanie—"

"I'm not going to leave my kid!" Edgar's mother insisted.

Ceese said quietly, "You're not leaving him. They'll be right behind us."

"I just have to pack a bag," Victoria said. "Edgar trusts me. Don't you, Edgar?"

All eyes were on him now. He had never seen anyone

stand up to his mother quite like this before.

"I'll go with Victoria," he said. It was just a few words, but they were his words to his mother, not the barking of some dog. He felt himself flush through. His mother could barely look at him. But she knew. *She knew.*

This was not really his fault at all.

"Go!" Victoria said to Ceese. "Tell the guys at the ice bridge to hold it open just a bit longer. *Go!*"

They were gone in a second. The door slammed shut. Caroline was left standing in the corner, her face a little shaky. "I'm with you two," she said in a small but steely voice.

RIVERBOAT

VICTORIA BEGAN MOVING RAPIDLY—
shoving clothes into a large duffel bag, calling someone
on the phone at the same time, then rushing to the fridge
to suddenly look at the state of her food, then coming
back to the duffel and phoning someone else.

She was trying to arrange somewhere to stay in town,
now that Ceese had betrayed her with Edgar's mother.

"We normally get a couple of days' notice when the
bridge is closing," Victoria said to him. "I'm normally not
running around like this!"

She wasn't running so much as lurching from one
thing to the next. Her phone whistled. It was Ceese.
"Where are you? They really are shutting down in just a
few minutes."

"We are almost in the goddamn truck. Don't call

again!" Victoria turned on Edgar. "Let's get your boots on."

It was getting light now. Edgar had been up much of the night. His body was warming. His hand was crinkling now from inside, tingling sharply. It hurt to move his fingers, but he could do it. The phone whistled again for Victoria. "Give me the keys!" Caroline said. "I'll start the truck!" Victoria threw them to her, and Caroline ran out the door.

Just to see, Edgar used his mouth to pull the sock off his right hand. His mitt came with it. The skin was red, red, but his fingers were more or less working. But oh, how they stung!

The other hand-sock came off easily.

He wouldn't rub, wouldn't rub the raw skin.

"Janey," Victoria said into her phone, "the bridge is closing soon. I have to run, but could you tell Des he could start looking after my dogs today? I was on my way over when all hell broke loose. Don't ask!"

Janey said something in return. She didn't have a huge voice like Ceese, so Edgar couldn't hear. When Victoria hung up, she hoisted the duffel onto her shoulders. "Let's go, let's go!" Finally she noticed. "Your fingers!"

Edgar moved them magically. She said, "Put the socks back on them, and let's go!"

Just as he was running out the door, Edgar noticed

three photos on the walls, all of hulking black ravens, looking on. And here was another one of a big black bear just raising his head, like the bear Edgar had walked to so stupidly just a few nights ago.

I'm sorry, Benjamin! he thought for the thousandth time.

Then the dogs exploded into such barking, they sounded like a load of gravel being dumped from a big truck.

"Oh, my lovelies!" Victoria called to them—a crowd of dogs running and yelping in the large, penned-off yard. "I'm sorry I'm going to leave without saying good-bye. But Des knows where the food is—"

They seemed to know what she was saying, and it only made them more anxious and excited.

(What *were* they saying? It just sounded like barking to Edgar. Maybe—maybe he had dreamed all of it, the dog-talking part especially.)

"Edgar!" Victoria called. "Come on!" She was heading to Ceese's truck, which was running. Edgar spied Caroline's face peering over the dashboard.

Maybe none of it had happened—the speaking drought, the long conversations with Benjamin.

"Edgar!" The truck engine revved.

"Edgar!"

He ran toward the truck. The dogs were barking, barking. They didn't want Victoria to go! Edgar called out, "Which one is Rupert?"

"Edgar, *come on!*" Victoria left the truck and ran to him. *"We have to—"*

That one there, the small brown one with the talkative eyes, that one must have been Rupert. He was telling Edgar, over and over, what had happened to Benjamin— or at least that was the sense that Edgar got, although he couldn't understand the actual words.

"I need to find Benjamin!" Edgar said.

Victoria grabbed him by the sleeve and pulled him over to the passenger side of the truck, lifted him in, and then slammed the door. Caroline had switched into the backseat. When Victoria got behind the wheel, Edgar held up his right hand and forced the fingers to open and close while he tried to keep his face calm.

"I think I'm okay," he said.

"That's great. But if I don't get you to the hospital, your mother will kill me!" Victoria threw the truck into reverse, and Edgar pitched forward in his seat. "Do up your seat belt!"

It was hard to turn and buckle while the truck bounced along the frozen lane between the trees.

"I need to find Benjamin," Edgar said again.

"Where is he?" Caroline said. "Where did you leave him?"

"We had an accident on the river, but I pulled him out," Edgar said. "He was freezing. We went to the Paddlewheel Graveyard, and then we got past the wolves and found Victoria's house."

"Wolves!"

"We can't look for him right now," Victoria said grimly. She seemed tough on the inside. But maybe that wasn't fair. Maybe anyone would be upset at Ceese and at Edgar's mother, and even at Edgar for showing up in the dark, trailing such dreadful news.

"But where is he now?" Caroline pressed.

"I thought he was with me," Edgar said in a little voice.

The truck bounced along a narrow, rocky road through the woods and then out onto a larger road, much more open. They turned and headed down a curve. Soon, there in the distance was the river, still mostly frozen, with large stretches of white, white snow and ice lined with black stretches—open water.

Had he and Benjamin really made their way across all that in the night?

A long line of trucks and cars was stopped at the point where the road met the ice bridge. Victoria crept up behind the last idling car.

"All right," she said, pushing her hair back off her forehead. "I think they'll let us across. They'll just stagger the vehicles to not stress the ice."

The town of Dawson sat, silent and still, on the other side while cars and trucks, well-spaced, navigated the snaking S-curve of the ice bridge.

Probably right where they were idling now was the very spot on the road where the wolf had sat sentinel, guarding passage to Victoria's house. For there was the smaller road heading down to the empty campsite, on the way to the Paddlewheel Graveyard.

"I think I know where Benjamin is," Edgar said.

Victoria hit a button on her door, and the truck locked shut around them.

"It's not far down that road," Edgar said, pointing.

"We have no time. I'm sorry." Victoria kept her eyes forward. Was she always this hard? She hadn't been the night of the band competition, when she'd sung that beautiful song, or in the photo shop, when she'd made all those prints for him.

"What, you mean he's down there?" Caroline said. "In the campground? I could run and get him."

"You're going nowhere. Neither of you. This is not a negotiation."

"But Benjamin is—"

"*No!*"

They waited, waited. A truck and then a car were allowed out onto the ice. The sun was rising, bright in the blue sky, and more vehicles lined up behind them. A bearded man in a dirty jacket knocked on Victoria's window. It seemed they knew each other.

"Are they going to strand us here, do you think?" the man said.

"I think we're okay. They're just being extra cautious," Victoria said.

The man gazed at Edgar. "Who's the boy?"

"Don't ask," Victoria said.

Waiting, more waiting. Edgar noticed workmen dressed in orange out on the ice, talking things over.

Victoria's phone buzzed. She peered at the screen, then touched some buttons.

"Your mother is worried," she said coldly.

"I'm sorry," Edgar said.

"Well, don't be. It's not your fault what adults do. Or do to you." She drummed her fingers on the steering wheel, then shut the engine off.

"It's not all your mom's fault either," Caroline said. "She's not the only one. My dad never learns. Why do you think *my* mom is in Whitehorse? Why do you think I'm here, with you guys? I mean, my dad is great, except when he's not." She looked more than a little angry, ready to burst out of her skin.

"I could've stayed in bed," Edgar said. "Benjamin knew better but still came after me. I should've been the one to fall through." Edgar told them more about the ice and the water, and nearly freezing, and losing his camera.

"That's a shame," Victoria said. "It was a beautiful instrument. But you made the right choice. A camera can be replaced. Your life—"

"Benjamin brought me to the Paddlewheel Graveyard because he smelled fire," Edgar said. "That's where he wanted to go. I think it's his favorite spot."

"It's just down there." Caroline pointed along the campsite road.

"I know," Edgar answered.

A few more cars were allowed to go onto the ice, slowly, slowly. Victoria restarted the engine and let the truck advance slightly down the hill. She seemed to be thinking, thinking.

"Nobody ever came after me before," Edgar said. "Nobody ever looked out for me."

"Your mother did," Victoria said.

Edgar looked at her. Yes, he supposed, she had come after him just now. She had tried to look after him in her way.

"I hate her guts at the moment," Victoria said, "but, you know, she is your mother."

"Yes," Edgar allowed.

"I mean, I really hate her. She saw a vulnerability, and she went for it. Ceese is a blockhead for falling the way he did. I guess I saw it happening, and I didn't want to see. And I guess it's some kind of blessing I found out now. I mean, we're not married. Caroline, you know—I still love you."

"And we all still love Benjamin!" Caroline said. "He might just be lying in the cold. You know it's not very far—"

Victoria shook her head; she swore to herself. Then, to Edgar, "Show me your hands again!"

Edgar pulled off the warm socks, and Victoria felt his fingers gently.

"The feeling is coming back?"

Edgar pretended he was playing a piano. Victoria looked at him, and then back at Caroline. "Oh crap!" She turned the wheel and steered them out of line and down the narrow lane on the other side of the road.

Victoria drove them to the end of the campsite road and then they got out. It really wasn't very far in the truck, in the daylight. It looked like a completely different place. Edgar knew the trail to the river, though, and walked ahead, Caroline right beside him. It wasn't so cold now. If the snow had been fresh, instead of old and frozen hard in the shadows, he would've been able to see his own footprints, and Benjamin's prints, going back and forth. But now he couldn't even smell the trail he and Benjamin must've left.

He was a boy again, just so.

At the river he ran toward the black spot in the distance. The smudge onshore grew and grew as he got closer. Caroline was running too, her arms pumping. "Benjamin!" she yelled. But Benjamin . . . Benjamin was not going to get up. He was lying by the old fire, the bits of charcoaled logs that had been so cold and disappointing in the night.

He was still, still. Not going to get up.

Edgar threw himself by his old friend, whose black hair remained hardened in spikes, whose eyes were frozen open and glassy.

No collar.

"Oh, Benjamin! Oh—" Caroline wailed.

And there were the dinosaur bones of the old paddle wheels, rising up out of the snow, whose ghostly outline Edgar had seen in the night.

Now he could see no wolf marks—no torn throat, no signs of battle or struggle.

Victoria approached from behind. "Ah, Benjamin!"

"He wanted to stay here," Edgar said. "But I forced him up so that he would walk with me to your house. He talked to the wolves; he made sure I knew the way and wasn't scared. And yet here he is. Here he is!"

"I didn't see him at all," Victoria said. "Are you sure he was with you? Are you sure there were wolves?"

Well, of course Benjamin had been with him, somehow. Of course there had been wolves! The big one in the woods and on the road, and so many others silvery in the shadows. Hadn't her own dogs been barking insanely?

How would Edgar ever have found her house without Benjamin, without some part of his friend, anyway, deep inside him?

"We can't leave him here," Edgar said.

"No, no!" Caroline said. Tears were streaming down her cheeks. "We have to bury him!"

"Kids," Victoria said, and Edgar knew from the tone of her voice that the workmen would not hold the bridge open much longer. They could not wait, anyway. *Look at that sun.* Edgar could almost feel the river ice contracting.

Look at that sun, over Victoria's shoulder. Look at the way the hills plunge down. He could feel the surge of water underneath the frozen skin. The same current that had almost taken Benjamin when Edgar had been wandering, misunderstanding the weight of his own steps.

"Let's move him at least," Edgar said.

So they picked up the frozen form of Benjamin. He hardly seemed a dog anymore, he was so stiff and strange, and not light to carry. Edgar and Caroline held up the old dog's head, cradling him with one last embrace, while Victoria took the hind end. It wasn't far to the wreckage of the nearest big boat. Edgar made room in the broken boards, and then they laid Benjamin with his head supported, in a frame of graying timbers.

"It's no treat to bury anyone in permafrost," Victoria said. "But we'll come back and do it properly before too long."

She looked behind her, back in the direction of the truck and the closing ice bridge.

Edgar watched her. With Benjamin's body resting now before them, it seemed right to hold on to her hand, and to Caroline's, even with his own hurt hands wearing socks.

Maybe they could be like their own kind of family?

To Victoria he said, "I like the way you sang, and how you love your dogs, and you live in a beautiful house. And you know things, without having to say them."

"Edgar—"

He looked at Caroline now. Did she and Victoria feel it, rising out of the frozen earth right here, where Benjamin was lying in the ruins of an old riverboat? It was practically a fire. That river was not going to stay frozen much longer. Did they feel it?

"We need to go, kids."

But they didn't. They kept standing, and the fire from the frozen earth went through them all—it must have, or Victoria would have dragged them off—and Edgar knew his mother was waiting at the hospital, that she would swim between the ice floes, or steal a helicopter, to come get him. Eventually.

His mother did love him, in her way. She would be his mother forever. But he had crossed a wild and breaking river, and oh, how warm it felt to have it stretch for now between them.

A horn blared in the distance. What did that mean? Victoria turned her head. Caroline's face lit up.

"How does three weeks of beans sound to you two?" Victoria asked quietly.

"I am very good at making porridge," Edgar said.

Both Caroline and Victoria had eyes that were kindly, familiar, and they both had nearly the same hook to their noses, which his camera would have loved if it hadn't been lost now, on or under the ice. They looked like they should have been mother and daughter. So Edgar took a picture with his eyes, and let the sun soothe his cheek and theirs at the same time. They didn't seem to be in a hurry anymore to get back to the truck, or to do anything in particular, now that the ice bridge was closed.

"Edgar, you are one hell of a charmer, I'll give you that," Victoria said. "The both of you, in cahoots!"

He was like his mother, Edgar supposed, who almost always got her way.

"You are both going to be real trouble when you get older!"

Would they? It was hard to imagine being older, being big.

Victoria was crying now. It was Edgar's fault, he felt. A lot had happened just overnight, and now it was hitting home.

Home. He would like to climb the ladder in Victoria's cabin. Did she have an extra bed up there? Probably he would just sleep on the couch.

She was crying, but she did not let go of their hands, so Edgar felt like he had done the right thing after all, or part of the right thing, in coming here.

"What's that?" he asked, looking across, not at Dawson but downriver to where some small buildings were poking out of the snow and woods.

"That's Moosehide Village," Caroline said.

And somehow that felt right too, that he was close to

where Chief Isaac had looked for safety with his people all those years ago.

"Would you sing something?" he asked Victoria.

She could not seem to help smiling through her crying. "What, now?"

Yes. Now. While Benjamin still seemed to be looking at them. She sang a song about a riverboat, how there was no road and the whole town flocked when the whistle blew, and who was at the wharf now, what had they brought? And how the waters churned, and the rapids sped, and the big rocks loomed, and the boilers steamed as the fire grew. And how the hills watched, the deep sky sighed, how the good folks eyed the stars from the deck in the steep black hard black night. The song went on and on. Victoria seemed to know dozens of verses, as the wheel kept churning, the fires burning, the big ship rounded, rounded the bend. Caroline, too, sang some of the verses. And Edgar hummed. He could hum. Maybe Victoria could teach him to sing? If they got only a day together, if it was only a week or three, she could still be his mother too, and Caroline could be his sister. They could sing together, why not? Why not? If he could talk to dogs, and cross the ice, and wander the woods at the direction of wolves?

Why couldn't the song just go on and on?

AUTHOR'S NOTE

I FELL IN LOVE WITH THE SPELL OF THE Yukon, the idea of the north, at an early age and from thousands of miles away, through the stories my father told from his geological exploration days, and through the work of Robert W. Service, Jack London, and others. I am deeply indebted to the Canadian Children's Book Centre, which sent me on a whirlwind tour of the Yukon in May 2012, and to the Writers' Trust of Canada, which opened the doors of the Berton House residency in Dawson City to me and my wife, Suzanne Evans, two years later. That's where the seeds of this particular story began to take root. I also gratefully acknowledge the support of the City of Ottawa through their Arts Funding Program, which helped finance a key draft.

Many thanks to early readers of the manuscript, including:

Ashleigh Elson, Helena Spector, Kathy Bergquist, Jasmine Murray-Bergquist, Suzanne Evans, Gwen Cumyn, Anna Cumyn, and Suzanne Cumyn. In Dawson City, special thanks to those at the Jack London Museum, the Robert Service Cabin, the Dänojà Zho Cultural Centre, the Dawson City Museum, Parks Canada, the Dawson City Community Library, the Klondike Visitors Association, and to the many friends and strangers, too numerous to list here, who went out of their way to share their stories of the place they call home. This novel is of course a work of fiction.

Segments of Jack London's 1908 short story "To Build a Fire," quoted here, are in the public domain in Canada and the United States, as are the lines quoted from Robert Service's 1907 poem "The Cremation of Sam McGee." I am also especially indebted to Helene Dobrowolsky's *Hammerstones: A History of the Tr'ondëk Hwëch'in* and to the Tr'ondëk Hwëch'in Heritage Sites' website for background information on Chief Isaac. The Chief Isaac quote about the catastrophic impact of the coming of the miners originally appeared in the *Dawson Daily News* December 15, 1911, and is reproduced on trondekheritage.com.

Heartfelt thanks to my agent, Ellen Levine, for early encouragement and guidance on the manuscript, and to my editor, Caitlyn Dlouhy, for loving Edgar and helping to steer this ship home. Finally, to my partner in exploring all things north and south, domestic and wild—Suzanne, this story simply would not be without you.